Praise for THE HEART OF A DOG

"As high-spirited as it is pointed. Unlike so much satire, it has a splendid sense of fun." —Eileen Battersby, *The Irish Times*

"Bulgakov here assaults the dour, utilitarian lives of Soviet citizens with a defiant, boisterous display of nonsense." —*The Times* (London)

"Spirited and entertaining." —*The Times Literary Supplement*

"As timely a piece of literary excellence as one could wish for ... The author is mordant and very funny. His style, through Michael Glenny's fine translation, has great strength and simplicity; the recommendation is unreserved." —*New Statesman*

"Such is Bulgakov's unobtrusive skill that it all seems quite believable ... The psychology is sound, the illusion is remarkably well sustained, the humor is never forced, and implicit always is a passionate and severe humanity." —*The New York Times Book Review*

"Bulgakov was unique, with a voice all his own ... Humorous rather than witty, horrifying rather than bitter, he was, in his daemonic fantasy and his uproarious laughter, akin to Gogol." —*The New York Review of Books*

THE HEART OF A DOG

MIKHAIL BULGAKOV (1891–1940) was born in Kiev. Schooled as a doctor, he gave up the practice of medicine in 1920 to devote himself to writing. He went on to write some of the greatest novels in twentieth-century Russian literature, including *The White Guard* and *Black Snow*. Though Bulgakov's work was often censored, Stalin showed his personal favor by protecting him from imprisonment and finding a job for him at the Moscow Art Theatre, where the writer would work as a director and playwright for many years. He died at the age of forty-nine from a kidney disorder. His masterpiece, *The Master and Margarita*, would not be published until twenty-six years after his death.

MICHAEL GLENNY (1927–1990) was at one point a British army officer, an intelligence agent in West Berlin, and a traveling salesman for Wedgwood china, which first took him to the Soviet Union. He eventually became most well-known as one of the world's leading translators of Russian literature, and particularly famous for bringing dissident writers to the fore, including Aleksandr Solzhenitsyn and Georgi Vladimov. He was the first to translate Mikhail Bulgakov into English, and his translations remain the definitive editions.

ANDREY KURKOV is a Ukrainian writer born in Russia. A linguist by training, he resisted pressure to be a KGB translator for his military service by opting instead to be a prison guard. Becoming a journalist afterward, he sold copies of his self-published books on the streets of Kiev until his career took off. Today, he is one of the most acclaimed and bestselling writers in Ukrainian history.

Also by Mikhail Bulgakov

A Country Doctor's Notebook
The White Guard
Black Snow

THE HEART OF A DOG

MIKHAIL BULGAKOV

translation and foreword by
MICHAEL GLENNY

introduction by
ANDREY KURKOV

 **MELVILLE HOUSE**
BROOKLYN · LONDON

THE HEART OF A DOG

Copyright © The Estate of Mikhail Bulgakov
English translation and translator's foreword
copyright © 1968 by The Harvill Press
Introduction copyright © 2009 by Andrey Kurkov

First Melville House printing: July 2013

Melville House Publishing   8 Blackstock Mews
145 Plymouth Street   and   Islington
Brooklyn, NY 11201   London N4 2BT

mhpbooks.com   facebook.com/mhpbooks   @melvillehouse

ISBN: 978-1-61219-288-8

Design by Christopher King

Printed in the United States of America
1 3 5 7 9 10 8 6 4 2

A catalog record for this title is available
from the Library of Congress.

Introduction

by ANDREY KURKOV

Mikhail Bulgakov got lucky as a writer only after his death. His was an unstable life, full of tightly shut doors. His attempts to avoid fighting in the civil war of 1918 to 1920 failed. The war always caught up with him. He was conscripted as a doctor for the army of the temporarily independent Ukrainian Republic. When he ran away to the Caucasus he was mobilized as a doctor for the White Guard, and by the end of the civil war he was in the Red Army. Eventually he decided that his only choice was to somehow muddle through in the new Soviet reality. His resolve was weak and his attempt to assimilate unsuccessful. While in the Caucasus, Bulgakov had planned to emigrate from the war-torn country. His failure to carry out that plan must have cast a dark shadow over his vision of the future.

In 1921, Bulgakov was living in Moscow and writing reports, satirical articles and reviews for several publications, including the proletarian newspapers *Gudok* and *Rabotchiy* (*The Worker*). Through his articles he learned to laugh at the young Soviet country without arousing anyone's ire. Censorship was in its infancy and barely active, and in one newspaper alone, over the course of a few years, he was able to publish around 120 satirical pieces and commentaries. But this genre was too restricting for Bulgakov. He wanted to go deeper, broader. He had seen so much during the years of revolution and civil war, experienced so much, understood so much! From 1923 to 1924 he wrote *The White Guard*, a collection of stories, *Diaboliad*, and the novella *The Fatal Eggs*. His first book was published and noted by both readers and critics.

Then in 1925 he wrote *The Heart of a Dog*, naïvely imagining that he would be able to publish this work too. But by 1925 censorship was maturing and so was the People's Commissariat for Internal Affairs (NKVD). Writers were now being watched, their conversations noted down. Writers with bourgeois backgrounds were, of course, the NKVD's first concern and Bulgakov certainly fell into that category. His father had been a lecturer at the Kiev Theological Academy and his mother a teacher at the aristocratic preparatory school. The long arms of the secret police would reach proletarian writers only later.

The manuscript of *The Heart of a Dog* had not reached the publisher when Bulgakov's flat was searched and the manuscript confiscated. It would not be published until 1968, twenty-eight years after the writer's death. From the moment of that first search, Bulgakov's life changed radically. He was trashed in the Soviet press. During his lifetime, not one more of his books would be published. He tried to earn a living by writing stage plays. Some were produced, but many were not. Bulgakov and his wife often went hungry, with no means to buy food. Bulgakov wrote to Maxim Gorky and members of the Politburo, asking them to arrange some employment for him or let him go and live abroad.

Eventually Bulgakov wrote Stalin himself asking for any kind of work at all, even as an assistant to a theatre director. And here the mystical quality of Bulgakov's work seems to transfer into the writer's own reality. A few days later, he received a phone call from Joseph Stalin himself. Stalin enquired as to how things were going for the writer. Bulgakov listed all his complaints and asked for help to find work. Stalin himself arranged to get Bulgakov a job as an assistant director at the Maly Teatr.

The strange relationship between Stalin and Bulgakov has always fascinated me. Stalin read and publicly criticized Bulgakov's prose and plays and yet he never sought his physical destruction. Bulgakov was never denounced as an 'enemy of the people.' He was never arrested and sent to a concentration camp. One of Bulgakov's last plays, *Batum*, was about Stalin's revolutionary activities as a young man. Stalin personally banned the play, declaring that Bulgakov was trying to win him over. If rumour is to be believed, then Stalin had actually taken offence at Bulgakov's portrayal of him as too gentle and kind.

From 1928 until the very end of his life, Bulgakov wrote and rewrote his most famous novel, *The Master and Margarita*. He never did finish rewriting it. *The Heart of a Dog*, on the other hand, has reached us as a finished work and, in this wonderfully angry novel, we see the Soviet Union of the 1920s, led by illiterate cooks and caretakers. We also glimpse the remains of pre-revolutionary Russia, for which the writer clearly felt a great sense of loss. Here too we see Bulgakov himself: the doctor-writer examining the country as he might examine a very sick and dangerous patient. The physician's gaze is stern, yet a little misty, as the one-time morphine addict adorns reality with his vivid imagination.

Andrey Kurkov
2009

Foreword

by MICHAEL GLENNY

According to the date on the typescript, Mikhail Bulgakov wrote *The Heart of a Dog* between January and March 1925. At this time he was earning a living as a freelance journalist, mostly writing feature articles and humorous stories for a wide selection of newspapers and magazines that ranged from the Petrograd edition of *Pravda* to medical journals and trade-union papers. It was a tough apprenticeship for a writer, similar to the early careers of Mark Twain and Rudyard Kipling. As with both these writers, it developed in Bulgakov a great mastery of the extended short story or novella; for circulation reasons, many editors wanted to run a story in installments in order to maintain reader interest over several issues. Bulgakov did not appreciate its educative value, however. To him it was just a grind to which he had to submit in order to keep paying the rent, and which he loathed. He hated having to truckle to editors and tone down his pieces for the censorship, hated having to write to order and hated tailoring his work to different kinds of readers, most of whom did not seem to want to read the sort of thing he wanted to write.

His real aim was to escape from the life of a hack and to be a "real" writer. A journalist by day, Bulgakov had been writing a novel "by moonlight." Based on his personal experiences as a doctor in Kiev during the civil war, it was called *The White Guard*. After many disappointments, it was accepted by a literary monthly called *Rossiya (Russia)* and the first two-thirds of the novel were published in the issues for April and May 1925. *Rossiya* folded before the final installment appeared, and the complete novel was not published in the Soviet Union until 1965. But those two installments had caught the eye of Pavel Alexandrovich Markov, the literary editor of the Moscow Art Theatre, who was on the lookout for contemporary literature suitable for dramatization. With Markov's help, Bulgakov turned *The White Guard* into a play. Retitled *The Days of the Turbins* and produced by the Moscow Art Theatre in 1926 with great success, this play made Bulgakov's reputation and is in the Soviet repertory to this day.

From then until his early death in 1940 at the age of forty-nine, Bulgakov made his career in the theatre. Although the censor kept many of his plays off the stage during his lifetime, and despite setbacks and disagreements with his producers, Bulgakov was a gifted and prolific dramatist who is at last being given his due in the Soviet theatre.

Owing to the fact that his early novel *The White Guard* and his many stories of fantasy and satire were never reprinted in his lifetime, until recently Bulgakov has been known largely as a playwright. During the last few years, however, a Soviet literary commission has been at work on his hitherto unpublished writings. This has led to the appearance in quick succession of two novels, a biography of Molière and the series of fascinating sketches based on Bulgakov's own early career as a country doctor. One of the novels was the extraordinary tour de force known as *The Master and Margarita*, a rich and complex work in which Bulgakov mixes profound philosophical speculation with fantasy and biting satire.

This great novel, which took ten years to write (1929–1939), began as a series of satirical sketches, a popular Russian genre in the twenties of which perhaps the most famous exponents were Ilf and Petrov, joint authors of *The Twelve Chairs* and *The Little Golden Calf*. It is interesting that during his journalistic career Bulgakov worked with Ilf and Petrov. At all events, he published a number of novella-length stories in the mid-twenties, often of a weird, disturbing nature that contained hints of malevolent supernatural forces at work in the confused affairs of modern man. His method in these stories, which he was later to expand and develop in *The Master and Margarita*, was one of "fantastic realism" in which frightening and often outrageously grotesque ideas are embodied in a narrative of straight, deadpan naturalism, a method which brilliantly sharpens the contrast between form and content. *The Heart of a Dog* is one of the best examples of this technique. Although a relatively early work, it is as mature, polished and ironic in style as any of Bulgakov's later writing. So far, however, it has not been published in the USSR; even today its tone is too sharp and its message too uncomfortable for the Soviet censor.

Like all the best satire, *The Heart of a Dog* can be read and relished in several ways: On one level it is a comic story of splendid absurdity; it also pokes fun at the discomforts, shortages and anomalies of life in the Moscow of the twenties. But it has more profound meanings. It is a fierce parable about the Russian Revolution. The "dog" of the story is the Russian people, brutalized and exploited for centuries—treated, in fact, like animals instead of human beings. The weird surgeon, a specialist in rejuvenation (for "rejuvenation," read "revolution"), is the embodiment of the Communist party—perhaps Lenin himself—and the drastic transplant operation that he performs in order to transform the dog into the simulacrum of a human being is the revolution itself. In the story, this modern Frankenstein is so appalled by the unredeemable beastliness of the creature he has conjured up that he reverses the process and turns his "new man" back into a dog. With this ending Bulgakov implies that he would like to see the whole ghastly experiment of the Revolution cancelled out; unfortunately, successful revolutionaries, even when they realize their mistake, cannot reverse history by a stroke of the pen as an artist can with his fictional creatures. The bitter message is that the Russian intelligentsia, which made the Revolution, is henceforth doomed to live with—and eventually to be ruled by—the crude, unstable and potentially brutal race of hominids—*homo sovieticus*—which it has called into being. Bulgakov saw the Revolution as a hideously misguided attempt to achieve the impossible—to change humankind. Man is brutish by nature, and "Soviet man," he warns, is little more than a lout who has been led to believe that he is the very pinnacle of creation. The results of giving power to such men will be disastrous; in fact, Stalin's terror was carried out ten years later by exactly the sort of callous, brutal cretins that Bulgakov satirizes in this grimly prophetic story.

April 1968

THE HEART OF A DOG

One

Ooow-ow-ooow-owow! Oh, look at me, I'm dying. There's a snowstorm moaning a requiem for me in this doorway and I'm howling with it. I'm finished. Some bastard in a dirty white cap—the cook in the office canteen at the National Economic Council—spilled some boiling water and scalded my left side. Filthy swine—and a proletarian, too. Christ, it hurts! That boiling water scalded me right through to the bone. I can howl and howl, but what's the use?

What harm was I doing him, anyway? I'm not robbing the National Economic Council's food supply if I go foraging in their dustbins, am I? Greedy pig! Just take a look at his ugly mug—it's almost fatter than he is. Hard-faced crook. Oh, people, people. It was midday when that fool doused me with boiling water, now it's getting dark, must be about four o'clock in the afternoon judging by the smell of onion coming from the Prechistenka fire station. Firemen have soup for supper, you know. Not that I care for it myself. I can manage without soup—don't like mushrooms either. The dogs I know in Prechistenka Street, by the way, tell me there's a restaurant in Neglinny Street where they get the chef's special every day—mushroom stew with relish at three roubles and seventy-five kopecks the portion. All right for connoisseurs, I suppose. I think eating mushrooms is about as tasty as licking a pair of galoshes . . . Oow-owowow . . .

My side hurts like hell and I can see just what's going to become of me. Tomorrow it will break out in ulcers and then how can I make them heal? In summer you can go and roll in Sokolniki Park where there's a special grass that does you good. Besides, you can get a free meal of sausage-ends and there's plenty of greasy bits of food-wrappings to lick. And if it wasn't for some old groaner singing 'O celeste Aïda' out in the moonlight till it makes you sick, the place would be perfect. But where can I go now? Haven't I been kicked around enough? Sure I have. Haven't I had enough bricks thrown at me? Plenty . . . Still, after what I've been through, I can take a lot. I'm only whining now because of the pain and cold— though I'm not licked yet . . . it takes a lot to keep a good dog down.

But my poor old body's been knocked about by people once too often. The trouble is that when that cook doused me with boiling water it scalded through right under my fur and now there's nothing to keep the cold out on my left side. I could easily get pneumonia—and if I get that, citizens, I'll die of hunger. When you get pneumonia the only thing to do is to lie up under someone's front doorstep, and then who's going to run round the dustbins looking for food for a sick bachelor dog? I shall get a chill on my lungs, crawl on my belly till I'm so weak that it'll only need one poke of someone's stick to finish me off. And the dustmen will pick me up by the legs and sling me on to their cart . . .

Dustmen are the lowest form of proletarian life. Humans' rubbish is the filthiest stuff there is. Cooks vary—for instance, there was Vlas from Prechistenka, who's dead now. He saved I don't know how many dogs' lives, because when you're sick you've simply got to be able to eat and keep your strength up. And when Vlas used to throw you a bone there

4

was always a good eighth of an inch of meat on it. He was a great character, God rest his soul, a gentleman's cook who worked for Count Tolstoy's family and not for your stinking Food Rationing Board. As for the muck they dish out there as rations, well it makes even a dog wonder. They make soup out of salt beef that's gone rotten, the cheats. The poor fools who eat there can't tell the difference. It's just grab, gobble and gulp.

A typist on salary scale 9 gets sixty roubles a month. Of course her lover keeps her in silk stockings, but think what she has to put up with in exchange for silk. He won't just want to make the usual sort of love to her, he'll make her do it the French way. They're a lot of bastards, those Frenchmen, if you ask me—though they know how to stuff their guts all right, and red wine with everything. Well, along comes this little typist and wants a meal. She can't afford to go into the restaurant on sixty roubles a month and go to the cinema as well. And the cinema is a woman's one consolation in life. It's agony for her to have to choose a meal . . . just think: forty kopecks for two courses, and neither of them is worth more than fifteen because the manager has pocketed the other twenty-five kopecks' worth. Anyhow, is it the right sort of food for her? She's got a patch on the top of her right lung, she's having her period, she's had her pay docked at work and they feed her with any old muck at the canteen, poor girl . . . There she goes now, running into the doorway in her lover's stockings. Cold legs, and the wind blows up her belly because even though she has some hair on it like mine she wears such cold, thin, lacy little pants—just to please her lover. If she tried to wear flannel ones he'd soon bawl her out for looking a frump. 'My girl bores me', he'll say, 'I'm fed up with those flannel knickers of hers, to hell with her. I've made good now and all I make in graft goes on women, lobsters and champagne. I went hungry often enough as a kid. So what—you can't take it with you.'

I feel sorry for her, poor thing. But I feel a lot sorrier for myself. I'm not saying it out of selfishness, not a bit, but because you can't compare us. She at least has a warm home to go to, but what about me? . . . Where can I go? Oowow-owow!

'Here, doggy, here, boy! Here, Sharik . . . What are you whining for, poor little fellow? Did somebody hurt you, then?'

The terrible snowstorm howled around the doorway, buffeting the girl's ears. It blew her skirt up to her knees, showing her fawn stockings and a little strip of badly washed lace underwear, drowned her words and covered the dog in snow.

'My God . . . what weather . . . ugh . . . And my stomach aches. It's that awful salt beef. When is all this going to end?'

Lowering her head the girl launched into the attack and rushed out of the doorway. On the street the violent storm spun her like a top, then a whirlwind of snow spiralled around her and she vanished.

But the dog stayed in the doorway. His scalded flank was so painful that he pressed himself against the cold wall, gasping for breath, and decided not to move from the spot. He would die in the doorway. Despair overcame him. He was so bitter and sick at heart, so lonely and terrified that little dog's tears, like pimples, trickled down from his eyes, and at once dried up. His injured side was covered with frozen, dried blood-clots and between them peeped the angry red patches of the scald. All the fault of that vicious, thick-headed, stupid cook. 'Sharik' she had called him . . . What a name to choose! Sharik is the sort of name for a round, fat, stupid dog that's fed on porridge, a dog with a pedigree, and he was a tattered, scraggy, filthy stray mongrel with a scalded side.

Across the street the door of a brightly lit store slammed and a citizen came through it. Not a comrade, but a citizen, or even more likely—a gentleman. As he came closer it was obvious that he was a gentleman. I suppose you thought I recognized him by his overcoat? Nonsense. Lots of proletarians even wear overcoats nowadays. I admit they don't usually have collars like this one, of course, but even so you can sometimes be mistaken at a distance. No, it's the eyes: you can't go wrong with those, near or far. Eyes mean a lot. Like a barometer. They tell you everything—they tell you who has a heart of stone, who would poke the toe of his boot in your ribs as soon as look at you—and who's afraid of you. The cowards—they're the ones whose ankles I like to snap at. If they're scared, I go for them. Serve them right ... grrr ... bow-wow ...

The gentleman boldly crossed the street in a pillar of whirling snow and headed for the doorway. Yes, you can tell his sort all right. He wouldn't eat rotten salt beef, and if anyone did happen to give him any he'd make a fuss and write to the newspapers—someone has been trying to poison me— me, Philip Philipovich.

He came nearer and nearer. He's the kind who always eats well and never steals, he wouldn't kick you, but he's not afraid of anyone either. And he's never afraid because he always has enough to eat. This man's a brain worker, with a carefully trimmed, sharp-pointed beard and grey moustaches, bold and bushy ones like the knights of old. But the smell of him, that came floating on the wind, was a bad, hospital smell. And cigars.

I wonder why the hell he wants to go into that Co-op? Here he is beside me ... What does he want? Oowow, owow ... What would he want to buy in that filthy store, surely he can afford to go to the Okhotny Ryad? What's that he's holding? Sausage. Look sir, if you knew what they put into that sausage you'd never go near that store. Better give it to me.

The dog gathered the last of his strength and crawled fainting out of the doorway on to the pavement. The blizzard boomed like gunfire over his head, flapping a great canvas billboard marked in huge letters, 'Is Rejuvenation Possible?'

Of course it's possible. The mere smell has rejuvenated me, got me up off my belly, sent scorching waves through my stomach that's been empty for two days. The smell that overpowered the hospital smell was the heavenly aroma of minced horsemeat with garlic and pepper. I feel it, I know— there's a sausage in his right-hand coat pocket. He's standing over me. Oh, master! Look at me. I'm dying. I'm so wretched, I'll be your slave for ever!

The dog crawled tearfully forward on his stomach. Look what that cook did to me. You'll never give me anything, though. I know these rich people. What good is it to you? What do *you* want with a bit of rotten old horsemeat? The Moscow State Food Store only sells muck like that. But you've a good lunch under your belt, haven't you, you're a world-famous figure thanks to male sex glands. Oowow-owow . . . What can I do? I'm too young to die yet and despair's a sin. There's nothing for it, I shall have to lick his hand.

The mysterious gentleman bent down towards the dog, his gold spectacle-rims flashing, and pulled a long white package out of his right-hand coat pocket. Without taking off his tan gloves he broke off a piece of the sausage, which was labelled 'Special Cracower'. And gave it to the dog. Oh, immaculate personage! Oowow-oowow!

'Here, doggy,' the gentleman whistled, and added sternly, 'Come on! Take it, Sharik!'

He's christened me Sharik too. Call me what you like. For this you can do anything you like to me.

In a moment the dog had ripped off the sausage-skin. Mouth watering, he bit into the Cracower and gobbled it down in two swallows. Tears started to his eyes as he nearly choked on the string, which in his greed he almost swallowed. Let me lick your hand again, I'll kiss your boots—you've saved my life.

'That's enough . . .' The gentleman barked as though giving an order. He bent over Sharik, stared with a searching look into his eyes and unexpectedly stroked the dog gently and intimately along the stomach with his gloved hand.

'Aha,' he pronounced meaningly. 'No collar. Excellent. You're just what I want. Follow me.' He clicked his fingers. 'Good dog!'

Follow you? To the end of the earth. Kick me with your felt boots and I won't say a word.

The street lamps were alight all along Prechistenka Street. His flank hurt unbearably, but for the moment Sharik forgot about it, absorbed by a single thought: how to avoid losing sight of this miraculous fur-coated vision in the hurly-burly of the storm and how to show him his love and devotion. Seven times along the whole length of Prechistenka Street as far as the cross-roads at Obukhov Street he showed it. At Myortvy Street he kissed his boot, he cleared the way by barking at a lady and frightened her into falling flat on the pavement, and twice he gave a howl to make sure the gentleman still felt sorry for him.

A filthy, thieving stray tom cat slunk out from behind a drainpipe and despite the snowstorm, sniffed the Cracower. Sharik went blind with rage at the thought that this rich eccentric who picked up injured dogs in doorways might take pity on this robber and make him share the sausage. So he bared his teeth so fiercely that the cat, with a hiss like a leaky hosepipe, shinned back up the drainpipe right to the second floor. Grrrr! Woof! Gone! We can't go handing out Moscow State groceries to all the strays loafing about Prechistenka Street.

The gentleman noticed the dog's devotion as they passed the fire station window, out of which came the pleasant sound of a French horn, and rewarded him with a second piece that was an ounce or two smaller.

Queer chap. He's beckoning to me. Don't worry, I'm not going to run away. I'll follow you wherever you like.

'Here, doggy, here, boy!'

Obukhov Street? OK by me. I know the place—I've been around.

'Here, doggy!'

Here? Sure . . . Hey, no, wait a minute. No. There's a porter on that block of flats. My worst enemies, porters, much worse than dustmen. Horrible lot. Worse than cats. Butchers in gold braid.

'Don't be frightened, come on.'

'Good evening, Philip Philipovich.'

'Good evening, Fyodor.'

What a character. I'm in luck, by God. Who *is* this genius, who can even bring stray dogs off the street past a porter? Look at the bastard—not a move, not a word! He looks grim enough, but he doesn't seem to mind, for all the gold braid on his cap. That's how it should be, too. Knows his place. Yes, I'm with this gentleman, so you can keep your hands to yourself. What's that—did he make a move? Bite him. I wouldn't mind a mouthful of horny proletarian leg. In exchange for the trouble I've had from all the other porters and all the times they've poked a broom in my face.

'Come on, come on.'

OK, OK, don't worry. I'll go wherever you go. Just show me the way. I'll be right behind you. Even if my side does hurt like hell.

From halfway up the staircase: 'Were there any letters for me, Fyodor?'

From below, respectfully: 'No sir, Philip Philipovich,' (dropping his voice and adding intimately), 'but they've just moved some more tenants into No. 3.'

The dog's dignified benefactor turned sharply round on the step, leaned over the railing and asked in horror: 'Wh-at?'

His eyes went quite round and his moustache bristled.

The porter looked upwards, put his hand to his lips, nodded and said: 'That's right, four of them.'

'My God! I can just imagine what it must be like in that apartment now. What sort of people are they?'

'Nobody special, sir.'

'And what's Fyodor Pavolovich doing?'

'He's gone to get some screens and a load of bricks. They're going to build some partitions in the apartment.'

'God—what is the place coming to?'

'Extra tenants are being moved into every apartment, except yours, Philip Philipovich. There was a meeting the other day; they elected a new house committee and kicked out the old one.'

'What will happen next? Oh, God . . . Come on, doggy.'

I'm coming as fast as I can. My side is giving me trouble, though. Let me lick your boot.

The porter's gold braid disappeared from the lobby. Past warm radiators on a marble landing, another flight of stairs and then—a mezzanine.

Two

Why bother to learn to read when you can smell meat a mile away? If you live in Moscow, though, and if you've got an ounce of brain in your head you can't help learning to read—and without going to night school either. There are forty thousand dogs in Moscow and I'll bet there's not one of them so stupid he can't spell out the word 'sausage'.

Sharik had begun by learning from colours. When he was just four months old, blue-green signs started appearing all over Moscow with the letters MSFS—Moscow State Food Stores—which meant a butcher and delicatessen. I repeat that he had no need to learn his letters because he could smell the meat anyway. Once he made a bad mistake: trotting up to a bright blue shop-sign one day when the smell was drowned by car exhaust, instead of a butcher's shop he ran into the Polubizner Brothers' electrical goods store on Myasnitzkaya Street. There the brothers taught him all about insulated cable, which can be sharper than a cabman's whip. This famous occasion may be regarded as the beginning of Sharik's education. It was here on the pavement that Sharik began to realize that 'blue' doesn't always mean 'butcher', and as he squeezed his burningly painful tail between his back legs and howled, he remembered that on every butcher's shop the first letter on the left was always gold or brown, bow-legged, and looked like a toboggan.

After that the lessons were rather easier. 'A' he learned from the barber on the corner of Mokhovaya Street, followed by 'B' (there was always a policeman standing in front of the last four letters of the word). Corner shops faced with tiles always meant 'CHEESE' and the black half-moon at the beginning of the word stood for the name of their former owners 'Chichkin'; they were full of mountains of red Dutch cheeses, salesmen who hated dogs, sawdust on the floor and reeking Limburger.

If there was accordion music (which was slightly better than 'Celeste Aïda'), and the place smelled of frankfurters, the first letters on the white signboards very conveniently spelled out the word 'NOOB', which was short for 'No obscene language. No tips.' Sometimes at these places fights would break out, people would start punching each other in the face with their fists—sometimes even with napkins or boots.

If there were stale bits of ham and mandarin oranges in the window it meant a grrr ... grrocery. If there were black bottles full of evil liquids it was ... li-li-liquor ... formerly Eliseyev Bros.

The unknown gentleman had led the dog to the door of his luxurious flat on the mezzanine floor and rung the doorbell. The dog at once looked up at a big, black, gold-lettered nameplate hanging beside a pink frosted-glass door. He deciphered the first three letters at once: P-R-O- 'Pro ...', but after that there was a funny tall thing with a cross bar which he did not know. Surely he's not a proletarian? thought Sharik with amazement ... He can't be. He lifted up his nose, sniffed the fur coat and said firmly to himself:

No, this doesn't smell proletarian. Some high-falutin' word, God knows what it means.

Suddenly a light flashed on cheerfully behind the pink

glass door, throwing the nameplate into even deeper shadow. The door opened soundlessly and a beautiful young woman in a white apron and lace cap stood before the dog and his master. A wave of delicious warmth flowed over the dog and the woman's skirt smelled of carnations.

This I like, thought the dog.

'Come in, Mr Sharik,' said the gentleman ironically and Sharik respectfully obeyed, wagging his tail.

A great multitude of objects filled the richly furnished hall. Beside him was a mirror stretching right down to the floor, which instantly reflected a second dirty, exhausted Sharik. High up on the wall was a terrifying pair of antlers, there were countless fur coats and pairs of galoshes and an electric tulip made of opal glass hanging from the ceiling.

'Where on earth did you get *that* from, Philip Philipovich?' enquired the woman, smiling as she helped to take off the heavy brown, blue-flecked fox-fur coat. 'God, he looks lousy.'

'Nonsense. He doesn't look lousy to me,' said the gentleman abruptly.

With his fur coat off he was seen to be wearing a black suit of English material; a gold chain across his stomach shone with a dull glow.

'Hold still, boy, keep still doggy ... keep still you little fool. Hm ... that's not lice ... Stand still, will you ... Hmm ... aha—yes ... It's a scald. Who was mean enough to throw boiling water over you, I wonder? Eh? Keep still, will you ...!'

It was that miserable cook, said the dog with his pitiful eyes and gave a little whimper.

'Zina,' ordered the gentleman, 'take him into the consulting room at once and get me a white coat.'

The woman whistled, clicked her fingers and the dog

followed her slightly hesitantly. Together they walked down a narrow, dimly lit corridor, passed a varnished door, reached the end, then turned left and arrived in a dark little room which the dog instantly disliked for its ominous smell. The darkness clicked and was transformed into blinding white which flashed and shone from every angle.

Oh, no, the dog whined to himself, you won't catch me as easily as that! I see it now—to hell with them and their sausage. They've tricked me into a dogs' hospital. Now they'll force me to swallow castor oil and they'll cut up my side with knives—well, I won't let them touch it.

'Hey—where are you trying to go?' shouted the girl called Zina.

The animal dodged, curled up like a spring and suddenly hit the door with his unharmed side so hard that the noise reverberated through the whole apartment. Then he jumped back, spun around on the spot like a top and in doing so knocked over a white bucket, spilling wads of cotton wool. As he whirled round there flashed past him shelves full of glittering instruments, a white apron and a furious woman's face.

'You little devil,' cried Zina in desperation, 'where d'you think you're going?'

Where's the back door? the dog wondered. He swung round, rolled into a ball and hurled himself bullet-fashion at a glass in the hope that it was another door. With a crash and a tinkle a shower of splinters fell down and a pot-bellied glass jar of some reddish-brown filth shot out and poured itself over the floor, giving off a sickening stench. The real door swung open.

'Stop it, you little beast,' shouted the gentleman as he rushed in pulling on one sleeve of his white coat. He seized the dog by the legs. 'Zina, grab him by the scruff of the neck, damn him.'

'Oh—these dogs . . . !'

The door opened wider still and another person of the male sex dashed in, also wearing a white coat. Crunching over the broken glass he went past the dog to a cupboard, opened it and the whole room was filled with a sweet, nauseating smell. Then the person turned the animal over on his back, at which the dog enthusiastically bit him just above his shoelaces. The person groaned but kept his head. The nauseating liquid choked the dog's breathing and his head began to spin, then his legs collapsed and he seemed to be moving sideways. This is it, he thought dreamily as he collapsed on to the sharp slivers of glass. Goodbye, Moscow! I shan't see Chichkin or the proletarians or Cracow sausages again. I'm going to the heaven for long-suffering dogs. You butchers—why did you have to do this to me? With that he finally collapsed on to his back and passed out.

When he awoke he felt slightly dizzy and sick to his stomach. His injured side did not seem to be there at all, but was blissfully painless. The dog opened a languid right eye and saw out of its corner that he was tightly bandaged all around his flanks and belly. So those sons of bitches did cut me up, he thought dully, but I must admit they've made a neat job of it.

'. . . "from Granada to Seville . . . those soft southern nights" . . .' a muzzy, falsetto voice sang over his head.

Amazed, the dog opened both eyes wide and saw two yards away a man's leg propped up on a stool. Trousers and sock had been rolled back and the yellow, naked ankle was smeared with dried blood and iodine.

Swine! thought the dog. He must be the one I bit, so that's my doing. Now there'll be trouble.

'... "the murmur of sweet serenades, the clink of Spanish blades ..." Now, you little tramp, why did you bite the doctor? Eh? Why did you break all that glass? Mm?'

Oowow, whined the dog miserably.

'All right, lie back and relax, naughty boy.'

'However did you manage to entice such a nervous, excitable dog into following you here, Philip Philipovich?' enquired a pleasant male voice, and a long knitted underpant lowered itself to the ground. There was a smell of tobacco, and glass phials tinkled in the closet.

'By kindness. The only possible method when dealing with a living creature. You'll get nowhere with an animal if you use terror, no matter what its level of development may be. That I have maintained, do maintain and always will maintain. People who think you can use terror are quite wrong. No, terror's useless, whatever its colour—white, red or even brown! Terror completely paralyses the nervous system. Zina! I bought this little scamp some Cracow sausage for one rouble forty kopecks. Please see that he is fed when he gets over his nausea.'

There was a crunching noise as glass splinters were swept up and a woman's voice said teasingly: 'Cracower! Goodness, you ought to buy him twenty kopecks' worth of scraps from the butcher. I'd rather eat the Cracower myself!'

'You just try! That stuff's poison for human stomachs. A grown woman and you're ready to poke anything into your mouth like a child. Don't you dare! I warn you that neither I nor Doctor Bormenthal will lift a finger for you when your stomach finally gives out ...'

Just then a bell tinkled all through the flat and from far away in the hall came the sound of voices. The telephone rang. Zina disappeared.

Philip Philipovich threw his cigar butt into the bucket, buttoned up his white coat, smoothed his bushy moustache in front of a mirror on the wall and called the dog.

'Come on, boy, you'll be all right. Let's go and see our visitors.'

The dog stood up on wobbly legs, staggered and shivered, but quickly felt better and set off behind the flapping hem of Philip Philipovich's coat. Again the dog walked down the narrow corridor, but saw that this time it was brightly lit from above by a round cut-glass lamp in the ceiling. When the varnished door opened he trotted into Philip Philipovich's study. Its luxury blinded him. Above all it was blazing with light: there was a light hanging from the moulded ceiling, a light on the desk, lights on the walls, lights on the glass-fronted cabinets. The light poured over countless knick-knacks, of which the most striking was an enormous owl perched on a branch fastened to the wall.

'Lie down,' ordered Philip Philipovich.

The carved door at the other end of the room opened and in came the doctor who had been bitten. In the bright light he now looked very young and handsome, with a pointed beard. He put down a sheet of paper and said: 'The same as before . . .'

Then he silently vanished and Philip Philipovich, spreading his coat-tails, sat down behind the huge desk and immediately looked extremely dignified and important.

No, this can't be a hospital, I've landed up somewhere else, the dog thought confusedly and stretched out on the patterned carpet beside a massive leather-covered couch. I wish I knew what that owl was doing here . . .

The door gently opened and in came a man who looked so extraordinary that the dog gave a timid yelp . . .

'Shut up! . . . My dear fellow, I hardly recognized you!'

Embarrassed, the visitor bowed politely to Philip Philipovich and giggled nervously.

'You're a wizard, a magician, professor!' he said bashfully.

'Take down your trousers, old man,' ordered Philip Philipovich and stood up.

Christ, thought the dog, what a sight!

The man's hair was completely green, although at the back it shaded off into a brownish tobacco colour; wrinkles covered his face yet his complexion was as pink as a boy's. His left leg would not bend and had to be dragged across the carpet, but his right leg was as springy as a jack-in-the-box. In the buttonhole of his superb jacket there shone, like an eye, a precious stone.

The dog was so fascinated that he even forgot his nausea. Oow-ow, he whined softly.

'Quiet! . . . How have you been sleeping!'

The man giggled. 'Are we alone, professor? It's indescribable,' said the visitor coyly. '*Parole d'honneur*—I haven't known anything like it for twenty-five years . . .' the creature started struggling with his fly buttons . . . 'Would you believe it, professor—hordes of naked girls every night. I am absolutely entranced. You're a magician.'

'Hm,' grunted Philip Philipovich, preoccupied as he stared into the pupils of his visitor's eyes. The man finally succeeded in mastering his fly buttons and took off his checked trousers, revealing the most extraordinary pair of pants. They were cream-coloured, embroidered with black silk cats and they smelled of perfume.

The dog could not resist the cats and gave such a bark that the man jumped.

'Oh!'

'Quiet—or I'll beat you! . . . Don't worry, he won't bite.'

Won't I? thought the dog in amazement.

Out of the man's trouser pocket a little envelope fell to the floor. It was decorated with a picture of a naked girl with flowing hair. He gave a start, bent down to pick it up and blushed violently.

'Look here,' said Philip Philipovich in a tone of grim warning, wagging a threatening finger, 'you shouldn't overdo it, you know.'

'I'm not overdo . . .' the creature muttered in embarrassment as he went on undressing. 'It was just a sort of experiment.'

'Well, what were the results?' asked Philip Philipovich sternly.

The man waved his hand in ecstasy. 'I swear to God, professor, I haven't known anything like it for twenty-five years. The last time was in 1899 in Paris, in the Rue de la Paix.'

'And why have you turned green?'

The visitor's face clouded over. 'That damned stuff! You'd never believe, professor, what those rogues palmed off on me instead of dye. Just take a look,' the man muttered, searching for a mirror. 'I'd like to punch him on the snout,' he added in a rage. 'What am I to do now, professor?' he asked tearfully.

'Hm. Shave all your hair off.'

'But, professor,' cried the visitor miserably, 'then it would only grow grey again. Besides, I daren't show my face at the office like this. I haven't been there for three days. Ah, professor, if only you had discovered a way of rejuvenating hair!'

'One thing at a time, old man, one thing at a time,' muttered Philip Philipovich. Bending down, his glittering eyes examined the patient's naked abdomen.

'Splendid, everything's in great shape. To tell you the truth I didn't even expect such results. You can get dressed now.'

' "Ah, she's so lovely . . ." ' sang the patient in a voice that quavered like the sound of someone hitting an old, cracked saucepan. Beaming, he started to dress. When he was ready he skipped across the floor in a cloud of perfume, counted out a heap of white banknotes on the professor's desk and shook him tenderly by both hands.

'You needn't come back for two weeks,' said Philip Philipovich, 'but I must beg you—be careful.'

The ecstatic voice replied from behind the door: 'Don't worry, professor.' The creature gave a delighted giggle and went.

The doorbell tinkled through the apartment and the varnished door opened, admitting the other doctor, who handed Philip Philipovich a sheet of paper and announced: 'She has lied about her age. It's probably about fifty or fifty-five. Heartbeats muffled.'

He disappeared, to be succeeded by a rustling lady with a hat planted gaily on one side of her head and with a glittering necklace on her slack, crumpled neck. There were black bags under her eyes and her cheeks were as red as a painted doll. She was extremely nervous.

'How old are you, madam?' enquired Philip Philipovich with great severity.

Frightened, the lady paled under her coating of rouge.

'Professor, I swear that if you knew the agony I've been going through . . . !'

'How old are you, madam?' repeated Philip Philipovich even more sternly.

'Honestly . . . well, forty-five . . .'

'Madam,' groaned Philip Philipovich, 'I'm a busy man.

Please don't waste my time. You're not my only patient, you know.'

The lady's bosom heaved violently. 'I've come to you, a great scientist ... I swear to you—it's terrible ...'

'How old are you?' Philip Philipovich screeched in fury, his spectacles glittering.

'Fifty-one!' replied the lady, wincing with terror.

'Take off your underwear, please,' said Philip Philipovich with relief, and pointed to a high white examination table in the corner.

'I swear, professor,' murmured the lady as with trembling fingers she unbuttoned the fasteners on her belt, 'this boy Moritz ... I honestly admit to you ...'

' "From Granada to Seville ..." ' Philip Philipovich hummed absentmindedly, and pressed the foot-pedal of his marble washbasin. There was a sound of running water.

'I swear to God,' said the lady, patches of real colour showing through the rouge on her cheeks, 'this will be my last affair. Oh, he's such a brute! Oh, professor! All Moscow knows he's a card-sharper and he can't resist any little tart of a dressmaker who catches his eye. But he's so deliciously young ...' As she talked the lady pulled out a crumpled blob of lace from under her rustling skirts.

A mist came in front of the dog's eyes and his brain turned a somersault. To hell with you, he thought vaguely, laying his head on his paws and closing his eyes with embarrassment. I'm not going to try and guess what all this is about—it's beyond me, anyway.

He was wakened by a tinkling sound and saw that Philip Philipovich had tossed some little shining tubes into a basin.

The painted lady, her hands pressed to her bosom, was

gazing hopefully at Philip Philipovich. Frowning impressively he had sat down at his desk and was writing something.

'I am going to implant some monkey's ovaries into you, madam,' he announced with a stern look.

'Oh, professor—not *monkey's?*'

'Yes,' replied Philip Philipovich inexorably.

'When will you operate?' asked the lady in a weak voice, turning pale.

' "... from Granada to Seville ..." Hm ... on Monday. You must go into hospital on Monday morning. My assistant will prepare you.'

'Oh, dear. I don't want to go into hospital. Couldn't you operate here, professor?'

'I only operate here in extreme cases. It would be very expensive—five hundred roubles.'

'I'll pay, professor!'

Again came the sound of running water, the feathered hat swayed out, to be replaced by a head as bald as a dinner-plate which embraced Philip Philipovich. As his nausea passed, the dog dozed off, luxuriating in the warmth and the sense of relief as his injury healed. He even snored a little and managed to enjoy a snatch of a pleasant dream—he dreamed he had torn a whole tuft of feathers out of the owl's tail ... until an agitated voice started yapping above his head.

'I'm too well known in Moscow, professor. What am I to do?'

'Really,' cried Philip Philipovich indignantly, 'you can't behave like that. You must restrain yourself. How old is she?'

'Fourteen, professor ... The scandal would ruin me, you see. I'm due to go abroad on official business any day now.'

'I'm afraid I'm not a lawyer ... you'd better wait a couple of years and then marry her.'

'I'm married already, professor.'

'Oh, lord!'

The door opened, faces changed, instruments clattered and Philip Philipovich worked on unceasingly.

This place is indecent, thought the dog, but I like it! What the hell can he want me for, though? Is he just going to let me live here? Maybe he's eccentric. After all, he could get a pedigree dog as easy as winking. Perhaps I'm good-looking! What luck. As for that stupid owl . . . cheeky brute.

The dog finally woke up late in the evening when the bells had stopped ringing and at the very moment when the door admitted some special visitors. There were four of them at once, all young people and all extremely modestly dressed.

What's all this? thought the dog in astonishment. Philip Philipovich treated these visitors with considerable hostility. He stood at his desk, staring at them like a general confronting the enemy. The nostrils of his hawk-like nose were dilated. The party shuffled awkwardly across the carpet.

'The reason why we've come to see you, professor . . .' began one of them, who had a six-inch shock of hair sprouting straight out of his head.

'You ought not to go out in this weather without wearing galoshes, gentlemen,' Philip Philipovich interrupted in a schoolmasterish voice. 'Firstly you'll catch cold and secondly you've muddied my carpets and all my carpets are Persian.'

The young man with the shock of hair broke off, and all four stared at Philip Philipovich in consternation. The silence lasted several minutes and was only broken by the drumming of Philip Philipovich's fingers on a painted wooden platter on his desk.

'Firstly, we're not gentlemen,' the youngest of them, with a face like a peach, said finally.

'Secondly,' Philip Philipovich interrupted him, 'are you a man or a woman?'

The four were silent again and their mouths dropped open. This time the shock-haired young man pulled himself together.

'What difference does it make, comrade?' he asked proudly.

'I'm a woman,' confessed the peach-like youth, who was wearing a leather jerkin, and blushed heavily. For some reason one of the others, a fair young man in a sheepskin hat, also turned bright red.

'In that case you may leave your cap on, but I must ask you, my dear sir, to remove your headgear,' said Philip Philipovich imposingly.

'I am not your dear sir,' said the fair youth sharply, pulling off his sheepskin hat.

'We have come to see you,' the dark shock-headed boy began again.

'First of all—who are 'we'?'

'We are the new management committee of this block of flats,' said the dark youth with suppressed fury. 'I am Shvonder, her name is Vyazemskaya and these two are comrades Pestrukhin and Sharovkyan. So we . . .'

'Are you the people who were moved in as extra tenants into Fyodor Pavlovich Sablin's apartment?'

'Yes, we are,' replied Shvonder.

'God, what is this place coming to!' exclaimed Philip Philipovich in despair and wrung his hands.

'What are you laughing for, professor?'

'What do you mean—laughing? I'm in absolute despair,' shouted Philip Philipovich. 'What's going to become of the central heating now?'

'Are you making fun of us, Professor Preobrazhensky?'

'Why have you come to see me? Please be as quick as possible. I'm just going in to supper.'

'We, the house management,' said Shvonder with hatred, 'have come to see you as a result of a general meeting of the tenants of this block, who are charged with the problem of increasing the occupancy of this house . . .'

'What d'you mean—charged?' cried Philip Philipovich. 'Please try and express yourself more clearly.'

'We are charged with increasing the occupancy.'

'All right, I understand! Do you realize that under the regulation of August 12 this year my apartment is exempt from any increase in occupancy?'

'We know that,' replied Shvonder, 'but when the general meeting had examined this question it came to the conclusion that taken all round you are occupying too much space. Far too much. You are living, alone, in seven rooms.'

'I live and work in seven rooms,' replied Philip Philipovich, 'and I could do with eight. I need a room for a library.'

The four were struck dumb.

'Eight! Ha, ha!' said the hatless fair youth. 'That's rich, that is!'

'It's indescribable!' exclaimed the youth who had turned out to be a woman.

'I have a waiting room, which you will notice also has to serve as my library, a dining room, and my study—that makes three. Consulting room—four, operating theatre—five. My bedroom—six, and the servant's room makes seven. It's not really enough. But that's not the point. My apartment is exempt, and our conversation is therefore at an end. May I go and have supper?'

'Excuse me,' said the fourth, who looked like a fat beetle.

'Excuse me,' Shvonder interrupted him, 'but it was just because of your dining room and your consulting room that we came to see you. The general meeting requests you, as a matter of labour discipline, to give up your dining room voluntarily. No one in Moscow has a dining room.'

'Not even Isadora Duncan,' squeaked the woman.

Something happened to Philip Philipovich which made his face turn gently purple. He said nothing, waiting to hear what came next.

'And give up your consulting room too,' Shvonder went on. 'You can easily combine your consulting room with your study.'

'Mm'h,' said Philip Philipovich in a strange voice. 'And where am I supposed to eat?'

'In the bedroom,' answered the four in chorus.

Philip Philipovich's purple complexion took on a faintly grey tinge.

'So I can eat in the bedroom,' he said in a slightly muffled voice, 'read in the consulting room, dress in the hall, operate in the maid's room and examine patients in the dining room. I expect that is what Isadora Duncan does. Perhaps she eats in her study and dissects rabbits in the bathroom. Perhaps. But I'm not Isadora Duncan . . . !' he turned yellow. 'I shall eat in the dining room and operate in the operating theatre! Tell that to the general meeting, and meanwhile kindly go and mind your own business and allow me to have my supper in the place where all normal people eat. I mean in the dining room—not in the hall and not in the nursery.'

'In that case, professor, in view of your obstinate refusal,' said the furious Shvonder, 'we shall lodge a complaint about you with higher authority.'

'Aha,' said Philip Philipovich, 'so that's your game, is it?'

And his voice took on a suspiciously polite note. 'Please wait one minute.'

What a man, thought the dog with delight, he's just like me. Any minute now and he'll bite them. I don't know how, but he'll bite them all right . . . Go on! Go for 'em! I could just get that long-legged swine in the tendon behind his knee . . . ggrrr . . .

Philip Philipovich lifted the telephone receiver, dialled and said into it: 'Please give me . . . yes . . . thank you. Put me through to Pyotr Alexandrovich, please. Professor Preobrazhensky speaking. Pyotr Alexandrovich? Hello, how are you? I'm so glad I was able to get you. Thanks, I'm fine. Pyotr Alexandrovich, I'm afraid your operation is cancelled. What? Cancelled. And so are all my other operations. I'll tell you why: I am not going to work in Moscow, in fact I'm not going to work in Russia any longer . . . I am just having a visit from four people, one of whom is a woman disguised as a man, and two of whom are armed with revolvers. They are terrorizing me in my own apartment and threatening to evict me.'

'Hey, now, professor . . .' began Shvonder, his expression changing.

'Excuse me . . . I can't repeat all they've been saying. I can't make sense of it, anyway. Roughly speaking they have told me to give up my consulting room, which will oblige me to operate in the room I have used until now for dissecting rabbits. I not only cannot work under such conditions—I have no right to. So I am closing down my practice, shutting up my apartment and going to Sochi. I will give the keys to Shvonder. He can operate for me.'

The four stood rigid. The snow was melting on their boots.

'Can't be helped, I'm afraid ... Of course I'm very upset, but ... What? Oh, no, Pyotr Alexandrovich! Oh, no. That I must flatly refuse. My patience has snapped. This is the second time since August ... What? Hm ... All right, if you like. I suppose so. Only this time on one condition: I don't care who issues it, when they issue it or what they issue, provided it's the sort of certificate which will mean that neither Shvonder nor anyone else can so much as knock on my door. The ultimate in certificates. Effective. Real. Armour-plated! I don't even want my name on it. The end.

'As far as they are concerned, I am dead. Yes, yes. Please do. Who? Aha ... well, that's another matter. Aha ... good. I'll just hand him the receiver. Would you mind,' Philip Philipovich spoke to Shvonder in a voice like a snake's, 'you're wanted on the telephone.'

'But, professor,' said Shvonder, alternately flaring up and cringing, 'what you've told him is all wrong—'

'Please don't speak to me like that.'

Shvonder nervously picked up the receiver and said: 'Hello. Yes ... I'm the chairman of the house management committee ... We were only acting according to the regulations ... the professor is an absolutely special case ... Yes, we know about his work ... We were going to leave him five whole rooms ... Well, OK ... if that's how it is ... OK.'

Very red in the face, he hung up and turned round.

What a fellow! thought the dog rapturously. Does he know how to handle them! What's his secret, I wonder? He can beat me as much as he likes now—I'm not leaving this place!'

The three young people stared open-mouthed at the wretched Shvonder.

'This is a disgrace!' he said miserably.

'If that Pyotr Alexandrovich had been here,' began the woman, reddening with anger, 'I'd have shown him . . .'

'Excuse me, would you like to talk to him now?' enquired Philip Philipovich politely.

The woman's eyes flashed.

'You can be as sarcastic as you like, professor, but we're going now . . . Still, as manager of the cultural department of this house . . .'

'Manager-*ess*,' Philip Philipovich corrected her.

'I want to ask you'—here the woman pulled a number of coloured magazines wet with snow, from out of the front of her tunic—'to buy a few of these magazines in aid of the children of Germany. Fifty kopecks a copy.'

'No, I will not,' said Philip Philipovich curtly after a glance at the magazines.

Total amazement showed on the faces, and the girl turned cranberry-colour.

'Why not?'

'I don't want to.'

'Don't you feel sorry for the children of Germany?'

'Yes, I do.'

'Can't you spare fifty kopecks?'

'Yes, I can.'

'Well, why won't you, then?'

'I don't want to.'

Silence.

'You know, professor,' said the girl with a deep sigh, 'if you weren't world-famous and if you weren't being protected by certain people in the most disgusting way' (the fair youth tugged at the hem of her jerkin, but she brushed him away), 'which we propose to investigate, you should be arrested.'

'What for?' asked Philip Philipovich with curiosity.

'Because you hate the proletariat!' said the woman proudly.

'You're right, I don't like the proletariat,' agreed Philip Philipovich sadly, and pressed a button. A bell rang in the distance. The door opened on to the corridor.

'Zina!' shouted Philip Philipovich. 'Serve the supper, please. Do you mind, ladies and gentlemen?'

Silently the four left the study, silently they trooped down the passage and through the hall. The front door closed loudly and heavily behind them.

The dog rose on his hind legs in front of Philip Philipovich and performed obeisance to him.

Three

On gorgeous flowered plates with wide black rims lay thin slices of salmon and soused eel; a slab of over-ripe cheese on a heavy wooden platter, and in a silver bowl packed around with snow—caviare. Beside the plates stood delicate glasses and three crystal decanters of different-coloured vodkas. All these objects were on a small marble table, handily placed beside the huge carved oak sideboard which shone with glass and silver. In the middle of the room was a table, heavy as a gravestone and covered with a white tablecloth set with two places, napkins folded into the shape of papal tiaras, and three dark bottles.

Zina brought in a covered silver dish beneath which something bubbled. The dish gave off such a smell that the dog's mouth immediately filled with saliva. The gardens of Semiramis! he thought as he thumped the floor with his tail.

'Bring it here,' ordered Philip Philipovich greedily. 'I beg you, Doctor Bormenthal, leave the caviare alone. And if you want a piece of good advice, don't touch the English vodka but drink the ordinary Russian stuff.'

The handsome Bormenthal—who had taken off his white coat and was wearing a smart black suit—shrugged his broad shoulders, smirked politely and poured out a glass of clear vodka.

'What make is it?' he enquired.

'Bless you, my dear fellow,' replied his host, 'it's pure alcohol. Darya Petrovna makes the most excellent homemade vodka.'

'But surely, Philip Philipovich, everybody says that thirty-degree vodka is quite good enough.'

'Vodka should be at least 40 degrees, not thirty—that's firstly,' Philip Philipovich interrupted him didactically, 'and secondly—God knows what muck they make into vodka nowadays. What do you think they use?'

'Anything they like,' said the other doctor firmly.

'I quite agree,' said Philip Philipovich and hurled the contents of his glass down his throat in one gulp. 'Ah ... mm ... Doctor Bormenthal—please drink that at once and if you ask me what it is, I'm your enemy for life. "From Granada to Seville ..." '

With these words he speared something like a little piece of black bread on his silver fish-fork. Bormenthal followed his example. Philip Philipovich's eyes shone.

'Not bad, eh?' asked Philip Philipovich, chewing. 'Is it? Tell me, doctor.'

'It's excellent,' replied the doctor sincerely.

'So I should think ... Kindly note, Ivan Arnoldovich, that the only people who eat cold *hors d'oeuvres* nowadays are the few remaining landlords who haven't had their throats cut. Anybody with a spark of self-respect takes his *hors d'oeuvres* hot. And of all the hot *hors d'oeuvres* in Moscow this is the best. Once they used to do them magnificently at the Slavyansky Bazaar restaurant. There, you can have some too.'

'If you feed a dog at table,' said a woman's voice, 'you won't get him out of here afterwards for love or money.'

'I don't mind. The poor thing's hungry.' On the point of

his fork Philip Philipovich handed the dog a titbit, which the animal took with the dexterity of a conjuror. The professor then threw the fork with a clatter into the slop-basin.

The dishes now steamed with an odour of lobster; the dog sat in the shadow of the tablecloth with the look of a sentry by a powder magazine as Philip Philipovich, thrusting the end of a thick napkin into his collar, boomed on:

'Food, Ivan Arnoldovich, is a subtle thing. One must know how to eat, yet just think—most people don't know how to eat at all. One must not only know what to eat, but when and how.' (Philip Philipovich waved his fork meaningfully.) 'And what to say while you're eating. Yes, my dear sir. If you care about your digestion, my advice is—don't talk about bolshevism or medicine at table. And, God forbid—never read Soviet newspapers before dinner.'

'Mmm . . . But there are no other newspapers.'

'In that case don't read any at all. Do you know I once made thirty tests in my clinic. And what do you think? The patients who never read newspapers felt excellent. Those whom I specially made read *Pravda* all lost weight.'

'Hm . . .' rejoined Bormenthal with interest, turning gently pink from the soup and the wine.

'And not only did they lose weight. Their knee reflexes were retarded, they lost appetite and exhibited general depression.'

'Good heavens . . .'

'Yes, my dear sir. But listen to me—I'm talking about medicine!'

Leaning back, Philip Philipovich rang the bell and Zina appeared through the cerise *portière*. The dog was given a thick, white piece of sturgeon, which he did not like, then immediately afterwards a chunk of underdone roast beef.

When he had gulped it down the dog suddenly felt that he wanted to sleep and could not bear the sight of any more food. Strange feeling, he thought, blinking his heavy eyelids, it's as if my eyes won't look at food any longer. As for smoking after they've eaten—that's crazy.

The dining room was filling with unpleasant blue smoke. The animal dozed, its head on its forepaws. 'Saint Julien is a very decent wine,' the dog heard sleepily, 'but there's none of it to be had any more.'

A dull mutter of voices in chorus, muffled by the ceiling and carpets, was heard coming from above and to one side.

Philip Philipovich rang for Zina. 'Zina my dear, what's that noise?'

'They're having another general meeting, Philip Philipovich,' replied Zina.

'What, again?' exclaimed Philip Philipovich mournfully. 'Well, this is the end of this house. I'll have to go away—but where to? I can see exactly what'll happen. First of all there'll be community singing in the evening, then the pipes will freeze in the lavatories, then the central heating boiler will blow up and so on. This is the end.'

'Philip Philipovich worries himself to death,' said Zina with a smile as she cleared away a pile of plates.

'How can I help it?' exploded Philip Philipovich. 'Don't you know what this house used to be like?'

'You take too black a view of things, Philip Philipovich,' objected the handsome Bormenthal. 'There is a considerable change for the better now.'

'My dear fellow, you know me, don't you? I am a man of facts, a man who observes. I'm the enemy of unsupported hypotheses. And I'm known as such not only in Russia but in Europe too. If I say something, that means that it is based on some fact from which I draw my conclusions. Now there's a fact for you: there is a hat-stand and a rack for boots and galoshes in this house.'

'Interesting . . .'

Galoshes—hell. Who cares about galoshes, thought the dog, but he's a great fellow all the same.

'Yes, a rack for galoshes. I have been living in this house since 1903. And from then until March 1917 there was not one case—let me underline in red pencil *not one case*—of a single pair of galoshes disappearing from that rack even when the front door was open. There are, kindly note, twelve flats in this house and a constant stream of people coming to my consulting rooms. One fine day in March 1917 all the galoshes disappeared, including two pairs of mine, three walking sticks, an overcoat and the porter's samovar. And since then the rack has ceased to exist. And I won't mention the boiler. The rule apparently is—once a social revolution takes place there's no need to stoke the boiler. But I ask you: why, when this whole business started, should everybody suddenly start clumping up and down the marble staircase in dirty galoshes and felt boots? Why must we now keep our galoshes under lock and key? And put a soldier on guard over them to prevent them from being stolen? Why has the carpet been removed from the front staircase? Did Marx forbid people to keep their staircases carpeted? Did Karl Marx say anywhere that the front door of No. 2 Kalabukhov House in Prechistenka Street must be boarded up so that people have to go round and come in by the back door? What good does it do anybody? Why can't the proletarians leave their galoshes downstairs instead of dirtying the staircase?'

'But the proletarians don't have any galoshes, Philip Philip-ovich,' stammered the doctor.

'Nothing of the sort!' replied Philip Philipovich in a voice of thunder, and poured himself a glass of wine. 'Hmm ... I don't approve of liqueurs after dinner. They weigh on the digestion and are bad for the liver ... Nothing of the sort! The proletarians do have galoshes now and those galoshes are—mine! The very ones that vanished in the spring of 1917. Who removed them, you may ask? Did I remove them? Impossible. The bourgeois Sablin?' (Philip Philipovich pointed upwards to the ceiling.) 'The very idea's laughable. Polozov, the sugar manufacturer?' (Philip Philipovich pointed to one side.) 'Never! You see? But if they'd only take them off when they come up the staircase!' (Philip Philipovich started to turn purple.) 'Why on earth do they have to remove the flowers from the landing? Why does the electricity, which to the best of my recollection has only failed twice in the past twenty years, now go out regularly once a month? Statistics, Doctor Bormenthal, are terrible things. You who know my latest work must realize that better than anybody.'

'The place is going to ruin, Philip Philipovich.'

'No,' countered Philip Philipovich quite firmly. 'No. You must first of all refrain, my dear Ivan Arnoldovich, from using that word. It's a mirage, a vapour, a fiction,' Philip Philipovich spread out his short fingers, producing a double shadow like two skulls on the tablecloth. 'What do you mean by ruin? An old woman with a broomstick? A witch who smashes all the windows and puts out all the lights? No such thing. What do you mean by that word?' Philip Philipovich angrily enquired of an unfortunate cardboard duck hanging upside down by the sideboard, then answered the question himself. 'I'll tell you what it is: if instead of operating every evening I were to start a glee club in my apartment, *that* would mean that I was on the road to ruin. If when I go to the lavatory I don't pee, if you'll excuse the expression, into the bowl but on to the floor instead and if Zina and Darya Petrovna were to do the same thing, the lavatory would be ruined. Ruin, therefore, is not caused by lavatories but is something that starts in people's heads. So when these clowns start shouting "Stop the ruin!"—I laugh!' (Philip Philipovich's face became so distorted that the doctor's mouth fell open.) 'I swear to you, I find it laughable! Every one of them needs to hit himself on the back of the head and then when he has knocked all the hallucinations out of himself and gets on with sweeping out backyards—which is his real job—all this "ruin" will automatically disappear. You can't serve two gods! You can't sweep the dirt out of the tram tracks *and* settle the fate of the Spanish beggars at the same time! No one can ever manage it, doctor—and above all it can't be done by people who are two hundred years behind the rest of Europe and who so far can't even manage to do up their own fly buttons properly!'

Philip Philipovich had worked himself up into a frenzy. His hawk-like nostrils were dilated. Fortified by his ample dinner he thundered like an ancient prophet and his hair shone like a silver halo.

His words sounded to the sleepy dog like a dull subterranean rumble. At first he dreamed uneasily that the owl with its stupid yellow eyes had hopped off its branch, then he dreamed about the vile face of that cook in his dirty white cap, then of Philip Philipovich's dashing moustaches sharply lit by electric light from the lampshade. The dreamy sleigh-ride came to an end as the mangled piece of roast beef, floating in gravy, stewed away in the dog's stomach.

He could earn plenty of money by talking at political meetings, the dog thought sleepily. That was a great speech. Still, he's rolling in money anyway.

'A policeman!' shouted Philip Philipovich. 'A policeman!'

Policeman? Ggrrr . . . —something snapped inside the dog's brain.

'Yes, a policeman! Nothing else will do. Doesn't matter whether he wears a number or a red cap. A policeman should be posted alongside every person in the country with the job of moderating the vocal outbursts of our honest citizenry. You talk about ruin. I tell you, doctor, that nothing will change for the better in this house, or in any other house for that matter, until you can make these people stop talking claptrap! As soon as they put an end to this mad chorus the situation will automatically change for the better.'

'You sound like a counter-revolutionary, Philip Philipovich,' said the doctor jokingly. 'I hope to God nobody hears you.'

'I'm doing no harm,' Philip Philipovich objected heatedly. 'Nothing counter-revolutionary in all that. Incidentally, that's a word I simply can't tolerate. What the devil is it supposed to mean, anyway? Nobody knows. That's why I say there's nothing counter-revolutionary in what I say. It's full of sound sense and a lifetime of experience.'

At this point Philip Philipovich pulled the end of his luxurious napkin out of his collar. Crumpling it up he laid it beside his unfinished glass of wine. Bormenthal at once rose and thanked his host.

'Just a minute, doctor,' Philip Philipovich stopped him and took a wallet out of his hip pocket. He frowned, counted out some white ten-rouble notes and handed them to the doctor, saying, 'You are due for forty roubles today, Ivan Arnoldovich. There you are.'

Still in slight pain from his dog-bite, the doctor thanked him and blushed as he stuffed the money into his coat pocket.

'Do you need me this evening, Philip Philipovich?' he enquired.

'No thanks, my dear fellow. We shan't be doing anything this evening. For one thing the rabbit has died and for another *Aïda* is on at the Bolshoi this evening. It's a long time since I heard it. I love it . . . Do you remember that duet? Pom-pom-ti-pom . . .'

'How *do* you find time for it, Philip Philipovich?' asked the doctor with awe.

'One can find time for everything if one is never in a hurry,' explained his host didactically. 'Of course if I started going to meetings and carolling like a nightingale all day long, I'd never find time to go anywhere'—the repeater in Philip Philipovich's pocket struck its celestial chimes as he pressed the button—'It starts at nine. I'll go in time for the second act. I believe in the division of labour. The Bolshoi's job is to sing, mine's to operate. That's how things should be. Then there'd be none of this "ruin" . . . Look, Ivan Arnoldovich, you must go and take a careful look: as soon as he's properly dead, take him off the table, put him straight into nutritive fluid and bring him to me!'

'Don't worry, Philip Philipovich, the pathologist has promised me.'

'Excellent. Meanwhile, we'll examine this neurotic street arab of ours and stitch him up. I want his flank to heal . . .'

He's worrying about me, thought the dog, good for him. Now I know what he is. He's the wizard, the magician, the sorcerer out of those dogs' fairy tales . . . I can't have dreamed it all. Or have I? (The dog shuddered in his sleep.) Any minute now I'll wake up and there'll be nothing here. No silk-shaded lamp, no warmth, no food. Back on the streets, back in the cold, the frozen asphalt, hunger, evil-minded humans ... the factory canteen, the snow ... God, it will be unbearable ... !

But none of that happened. It was the freezing doorway which vanished like a bad dream and never came back.

Clearly the country was not yet in a total state of ruin. In spite of it the grey accordion-shaped radiators under the windows filled with heat twice a day and warmth flowed in waves through the whole apartment. The dog had obviously drawn the winning ticket in the dogs' lottery. Never less than twice a day his eyes filled with tears of gratitude towards the sage of Prechistenka. Every mirror in the living room or the hall reflected a good-looking, successful dog.

I am handsome. Perhaps I'm really a dog prince, living incognito, mused the dog as he watched the shaggy, coffee-coloured dog with the smug expression strolling about in the mirrored distance. I wouldn't be surprised if my grandmother didn't have an affair with a labrador. Now that I look at my muzzle, I see there's a white patch on it. I wonder how it got there. Philip Philipovich is a man of great taste—he wouldn't just pick up any stray mongrel.

In two weeks the dog ate as much as in his previous six weeks on the street. Only by weight, of course. In quality the food at the professor's apartment was incomparable. Apart from the fact that Darya Petrovna bought a heap of meat-scraps for eighteen kopecks every day at the Smolensk market, there was dinner every evening in the dining room at seven o'clock, at which the dog was always present despite protests from the elegant Zina. It was during these meals that Philip Philipovich acquired his final title to divinity. The dog stood on his hind legs and nibbled his jacket, the dog learned to recognize Philip Philipovich's ring at the door—two loud, abrupt proprietorial pushes on the bell—and would run barking out into the hall. The master was enveloped in a dark brown fox-fur coat, which glittered with millions of snowflakes and smelled of mandarin oranges, cigars, perfume, lemons, petrol, *eau de cologne* and cloth, and his voice, like a megaphone, boomed all through the apartment.

'Why did you ruin the owl, you little monkey? Was the owl doing you any harm? Was it, now? Why did you smash the portrait of Professor Mechnikov?'

'He needs at least one good whipping, Philip Philipovich,' said Zina indignantly, 'or he'll become completely spoiled. Just look what he's done to your galoshes.'

'No one is to be beaten,' said Philip Philipovich heatedly, 'remember that once and for all. Animals and people can only be influenced by persuasion. Have you given him his meat today?'

'Lord, he's eaten us out of house and home. What a question, Philip Philipovich. He eats so much I'm surprised he doesn't burst.'

'Fine. It's good for him . . . what harm did the owl do you, you little ruffian?'

Ow-ow, whined the dog, crawling on his belly and splaying out his paws.

The dog was forcefully dragged by the scruff of his neck through the hall and into the study. He whined, snapped, clawed at the carpet and slid along on his rump as if he were doing a circus act. In the middle of the study floor lay the glass-eyed owl. From its disembowelled stomach flowed a stream of red rags that smelled of mothballs. Scattered on the desk were the fragments of a portrait.

'I purposely didn't clear it up so that you could take a good look,' said Zina distractedly. 'Look—he jumped up on to the table, the little brute, and then—bang!—he had the owl by the tail. Before I knew what was happening he had torn it to pieces. Rub his nose in the owl, Philip Philipovich, so that he learns not to spoil things.'

Then the howling began. Clawing at the carpet, the dog was dragged over to have his nose rubbed in the owl. He wept bitter tears and thought: Beat me, do what you like, but don't throw me out.

'Send the owl to the taxidermist at once. There's eight roubles, and sixteen kopecks for the tram fare, go down to Murat's and buy him a good collar and a lead.'

Next day the dog was given a wide, shiny collar. As soon as he saw himself in the mirror he was very upset, put his tail between his legs and disappeared into the bathroom, where he planned to pull the collar off against a box or a basket. Soon, however, the dog realized that he was simply a fool. Zina took him walking on the lead along Obukhov Street. The dog trotted along like a prisoner under arrest, burning with shame, but as he walked along Prechistenka Street as far as the church of Christ the Saviour he soon realized exactly what a collar means in life. Mad envy burned in the eyes of every dog he met and at Myortvy Street a shaggy mongrel with a docked tail barked at him that he was a 'master's pet' and a 'lackey'. As they crossed the tram tracks a policeman looked at the collar with approval and respect. When they returned home the most amazing thing of all happened—with his own hands Fyodor the porter opened the front door to admit Sharik and Zina, remarking to Zina as he did so: 'What a sight he was when Philip Philipovich brought him in. And now look how fat he is.'

'So he should be—he eats enough for six,' said the beautiful Zina, rosy-cheeked from the cold.

A collar's just like a briefcase, the dog smiled to himself. Wagging his tail, he climbed up to the mezzanine like a gentleman.

Once having appreciated the proper value of a collar, the dog made his first visit to the supreme paradise from which hitherto he had been categorically barred—the realm of the cook, Darya Petrovna. Two square inches of Darya's kitchen was worth more than all the rest of the flat. Every day flames roared and flashed in the tiled, black-leaded stove. Delicious crackling sounds came from the oven. Tortured by perpetual heat and unquenchable passion, Darya Petrovna's face was a constant livid purple, slimy and greasy. In the neat coils over her ears and in the blonde bun on the back of her head flashed twenty-two imitation diamonds. Golden saucepans hung on hooks round the walls, the whole kitchen seethed with smells, while covered pans bubbled and hissed . . .

'Get out!' screamed Darya Petrovna. 'Get out, you no-good little thief! Get out of here at once or I'll be after you with the poker!'

Hey, why all the barking? signalled the dog pathetically with his eyes. What d'you mean—thief? Haven't you noticed my new collar? He backed towards the door, his muzzle raised appealingly towards her.

The dog Sharik possessed some secret which enabled him to win people's hearts. Two days later he was stretched out beside the coal-scuttle watching Darya Petrovna at work. With a thin sharp knife she cut off the heads and claws of a flock of helpless grouse, then like a merciless executioner scooped the guts out of the fowls, stripped the flesh from the bones and put it into the mincer. Sharik meanwhile gnawed a grouse's head. Darya Petrovna fished lumps of soaking bread out of a bowl of milk, mixed them on a board with the minced meat, poured cream over the whole mixture, sprinkled it with salt and kneaded it into cutlets. The stove was roaring like a furnace, the frying pan sizzled, popped and bubbled. The oven door swung open with a roar, revealing a terrifying inferno of heaving, crackling flame.

In the evening the fiery furnace subsided and above the curtain half-way up the kitchen window hung the dense, ominous night sky of Prechistenka Street with its single star. The kitchen floor was damp, the saucepans shone with a dull, mysterious glow and on the table was a fireman's cap. Sharik lay on the warm stove, stretched out like a lion above a gateway, and with one ear cocked in curiosity he watched through the half-open door of Zina's and Darya Petrovna's room as an excited, black-moustached man in a broad leather belt embraced Darya Petrovna. All her face, except her powdered nose, glowed with agony and passion. A streak of light lay across a picture of a man with a black moustache and beard, from which hung a little Easter loaf.

'Don't go too far,' muttered Darya Petrovna in the half-darkness. 'Stop it! Zina will be back soon. What's the matter with you—have you been rejuvenated too?'

'I don't need rejuvenating,' croaked the black-moustached fireman hoarsely, scarcely able to control himself. 'You're so passionate!'

In the evenings the sage of Prechistenka Street retired behind his thick blinds and if there was no *Aïda* at the Bolshoi Theatre and no meeting of the All-Russian Surgical Society, then the great man would settle down in a deep armchair in his study. There were no ceiling lights; the only light came from a green-shaded lamp on the desk. Sharik lay on the carpet in the shadows, unable to take his eyes off the horrors that lined the room.

Human brains floated in a disgustingly acrid, murky liquid in glass jars. On his forearms, bared to the elbow, the great man wore red rubber gloves as his blunt, slippery fingers delved into the convoluted grey matter. Now and again he would pick up a small glistening knife and calmly slice off a spongey yellow chunk of brain.

'... "to the banks of the sa-acred Nile ...," ' he hummed quietly, licking his lips as he remembered the gilded auditorium of the Bolshoi Theatre.

It was the time of evening when the central heating was at its warmest. The heat from it floated up to the ceiling, from there dispersing all over the room. In the dog's fur the warmth wakened the last flea, which had somehow managed to escape Philip Philipovich's comb. The carpets deadened all sound in the flat. Then, from far away, came the sound of the front door bell.

Zina's gone out to the cinema, thought the dog, and I suppose we'll have supper when she gets home. Something tells me that it's veal chops tonight!

On the morning of that terrible day Sharik had felt a sense of foreboding, which had made him suddenly break into a howl, and he had eaten his breakfast—half a bowl of porridge and yesterday's mutton-bone—without the least relish. Bored, he went padding up and down the hall, whining at his own reflection. The rest of the morning, after Zina had taken him for his walk along the avenue, passed normally. There were no patients that day as it was Tuesday—a day when as we all know there are no consulting hours. The master was in his study, several large books with coloured pictures spread out in front of him on the desk. It was nearly supper-time.

The dog was slightly cheered by the news from the kitchen that the second course tonight was turkey. As he was walking down the passage the dog heard the startling, unexpected noise of Philip Philipovich's telephone bell ringing. Philip Philipovich picked up the receiver, listened and suddenly became very excited.

'Excellent,' he was heard saying, 'bring it round at once, at once!'

Bustling about, he rang for Zina and ordered supper to be served immediately: 'Supper! Supper!'

Immediately there was a clatter of plates in the dining room and Zina ran in, pursued by the voice of Darya Petrovna grumbling that the turkey was not ready yet. Again the dog felt a tremor of anxiety.

I don't like it when there's a commotion in the house, he mused ... and no sooner had the thought entered his head than the commotion took on an even more disagreeable nature. This was largely due to the appearance of Doctor Bormenthal, who brought with him an evil-smelling trunk and without waiting to remove his coat started heaving it down the corridor into the consulting room. Philip Philipovich put down his unfinished cup of coffee, which normally he would never do, and ran out to meet Bormenthal, another quite untypical thing for him to do.

'When did he die?' he cried.

'Three hours ago,' replied Bormenthal, his snow-covered hat still on his head as he unstrapped the trunk.

Who's died? wondered the dog sullenly and disagreeably as he slunk under the table. I can't bear it when they dash about the room like that.

'Out of my way, animal! Hurry, hurry, hurry!' cried Philip Philipovich.

It seemed to the dog that the master was ringing every bell at once. Zina ran in. 'Zina! Tell Darya Petrovna to take over the telephone and not to let anybody in. I need you here. Doctor Bormenthal—please hurry!'

I don't like this, scowled the dog, offended, and wandered off round the apartment. All the bustle, it seemed, was confined to the consulting room. Zina suddenly appeared in a white coat like a shroud and began running back and forth between the consulting room and the kitchen.

Isn't it time I had my supper? They seem to have forgotten about me, thought the dog. He at once received an unpleasant surprise.

'Don't give Sharik anything to eat,' boomed the order from the consulting room.

'How am I to keep an eye on him?'

'Lock him up!'

Sharik was enticed into the bathroom and locked in.

Beasts, thought Sharik as he sat in the semi-darkness of the bathroom. What an outrage . . . In an odd frame of mind, half resentful, half depressed, he spent about a quarter of an hour in the bathroom. He felt irritated and uneasy.

Right. This means the end of your galoshes tomorrow, Philip Philipovich, he thought. You've already had to buy two new pairs. Now you're going to have to buy another. That'll teach you to lock up dogs.

Suddenly a violent thought crossed his mind. Instantly and clearly he remembered a scene from his earliest youth—a huge sunny courtyard near the Preobrazhensky Gate, slivers of sunlight reflected in broken bottles, brick rubble, and a free world of stray dogs.

No, it's no use. I could never leave this place now. Why

pretend? mused the dog, with a sniff. I've got used to this life. I'm a gentleman's dog now, an intelligent being, I've tasted better things. Anyhow, what is freedom? Vapour, mirage, fiction . . . democratic rubbish . . .

Then the gloom of the bathroom began to frighten him and he howled. Hurling himself at the door, he started scratching it.

Ow-ow . . . , the noise echoed round the apartment like someone shouting into a barrel.

I'll tear that owl to pieces again, thought the dog, furious but impotent. Then he felt weak and lay down. When he got up his coat suddenly stood up on end, as he had an eerie feeling that a horrible, wolfish pair of eyes was staring at him from the bath.

In the midst of his agony the door opened. The dog went out, shook himself, and made gloomily for the kitchen, but Zina firmly dragged him by the collar into the consulting room. The dog felt a sudden chill around his heart.

What do they want me for? he wondered suspiciously. My side has healed up—I don't get it. Sliding along on his paws over the slippery parquet, he was pulled into the consulting room. There he was immediately shocked by the unusually brilliant lighting. A white globe on the ceiling shone so brightly that it hurt his eyes. In the white glare stood the high priest, humming through his teeth something about the sacred Nile. The only way of recognizing him as Philip Philipovich was a vague smell. His smoothed-back grey hair was hidden under a white cap, making him look as if he were dressed up as a patriarch; the divine figure was all in white and over the white, like a stole, he wore a narrow rubber apron. His hands were in black gloves.

The other doctor was also there. The long table was fully unfolded, a small square box placed beside it on a shining stand.

The dog hated the other doctor more than anyone else and more than ever because of the look in his eyes. Usually frank and bold, they now flickered in all directions to avoid the dog's eyes. They were watchful, treacherous and in their depths lurked something mean and nasty, even criminal. Scowling at him, the dog slunk into a corner.

'Collar, Zina,' said Philip Philipovich softly, 'only don't excite him.'

For a moment Zina's eyes had the same vile look as Bormenthal's. She walked up to the dog and with obvious treachery, stroked him.

What're you doing . . . all three of you? OK, take me if you want me. You ought to be ashamed . . . If only I knew what you're going to do to me . . .

Zina unfastened his collar, the dog shook his head and snorted. Bormenthal rose up in front of him, reeking of that foul, sickening smell.

Ugh, disgusting . . . wonder why I feel so queer . . . , thought the dog as he dodged away.

'Hurry, doctor,' said Philip Philipovich impatiently.

There was a sharp, sweet smell in the air. The doctor, without taking his horrible watchful eyes off the dog slipped his right hand out from behind his back and quickly clamped a pad of damp cotton wool over the dog's nose. Sharik went dumb, his head spinning a little, but he still managed to jump back. The doctor jumped after him and rapidly smothered his whole muzzle in cotton wool. His breathing stopped, but again the dog jerked himself away. You bastard . . . , flashed through his mind. Why? And down came the pad again.

Then a lake suddenly materialized in the middle of the consulting room floor. On it was a boat, rowed by a crew of extraordinary pink dogs. The bones in his legs gave way and collapsed.

'On to the table!' Philip Philipovich boomed from somewhere in a cheerful voice and the sound disintegrated into orange-coloured streaks. Fear vanished and gave way to joy. For two seconds the dog loved the man he had bitten. Then the whole world turned upside down and he felt a cold but soothing hand on his belly. Then—nothing.

The dog Sharik lay stretched out on the narrow operating table, his head lolling helplessly against a white oilcloth pillow. His stomach was shaven and now Doctor Bormenthal, breathing heavily, was hurriedly shaving Sharik's head with clippers that ate through his fur. Philip Philipovich, leaning on the edge of the table, watched the process through his shiny, gold-rimmed spectacles. He spoke urgently:

'Ivan Arnoldovich, the most vital moment is when I enter the Turkish saddle. You must then instantly pass me the gland and start suturing at once. If we have a haemorrhage then we shall lose time and lose the dog. In any case, he hasn't a chance . . .' He was silent, frowning, and gave an ironic look at the dog's half-closed eye, then added: 'Do you know, I feel sorry for him. I've actually got used to having him around.'

So saying he raised his hands as though calling down a blessing on the unfortunate Sharik's great sacrificial venture. Bormenthal laid aside the clippers and picked up a razor. He lathered the defenceless little head and started to shave it. The blade scraped across the skin, nicked it and drew blood. Having shaved the head the doctor wiped it with an alcohol swab, then stretched out the dog's bare stomach and said with a sigh of relief: 'Ready.'

Zina turned on the tap over the washbasin and Bormenthal hurriedly washed his hands. From a phial Zina poured alcohol over them.

'May I go, Philip Philipovich?' she asked, glancing nervously at the dog's shaven head.

'You may.'

Zina disappeared. Bormenthal busied himself further. He surrounded Sharik's head with tight gauze wadding, which framed the odd sight of a naked canine scalp and a muzzle that by comparison seemed heavily bearded.

The priest stirred. He straightened up, looked at the dog's head and said: 'God bless us. Scalpel.'

Bormenthal took a short, broad-bladed knife from the glittering pile on the small table and handed it to the great man. He too then donned a pair of black gloves.

'Is he asleep?' asked Philip Philipovich.

'He's sleeping nicely.'

Philip Philipovich clenched his teeth, his eyes took on a sharp, piercing glint and with a flourish of his scalpel he made a long, neat incision down the length of Sharik's belly. The skin parted instantly, spurting blood in several directions. Bormenthal swooped like a vulture, began dabbing Sharik's wound with swabs of gauze, then gripped its edges with a row of little clamps like sugar-tongs, and the bleeding stopped. Droplets of sweat oozed from Bormenthal's forehead. Philip Philipovich made a second incision and again Sharik's body was pulled apart by hooks, scissors and little clamps. Pink and yellow tissues emerged, oozing with blood. Philip Philipovich turned the scalpel in the wound, then barked: 'Scissors!'

Like a conjuring trick the instrument materialized in

Bormenthal's hand. Philip Philipovich delved deep and with a few twists he removed the testicles and some dangling attachments from Sharik's body. Dripping with exertion and excitement Bormenthal leapt to a glass jar and removed from it two more wet, dangling testicles, their short, moist, stringy vesicles dangling like elastic in the hands of the professor and his assistant. The bent needles clicked faintly against the clamps as the new testicles were sewn in place of Sharik's. The priest drew back from the incision, swabbed it and gave the order:

'Suture, doctor. At once.' He turned around and looked at the white clock on the wall.

'Fourteen minutes,' grunted Bormenthal through clenched teeth as he pierced the flabby skin with his crooked needle. Both grew as tense as two murderers working against the clock.

'Scalpel!' cried Philip Philipovich.

The scalpel seemed to leap into his hand as though of its own accord, at which point Philip Philipovich's expression grew quite fearsome. Grinding his gold and porcelain bridge-work, in a single stroke he incised a red fillet around Sharik's head. The scalp, with its shaven hairs, was removed, the skull bone laid bare. Philip Philipovich shouted: 'Trepan!'

Bormenthal handed him a shining auger. Biting his lips Philip Philipovich began to insert the auger and drill a complete circle of little holes, a centimetre apart, around the top of Sharik's skull. Each hole took no more than five seconds to drill. Then with a saw of the most curious design he put its point into the first hole and began sawing through the skull as though he were making a lady's fretwork sewing-basket. The skull shook and squeaked faintly. After three minutes the roof of the dog's skull was removed.

The dome of Sharik's brain was now laid bare—grey, threaded with bluish veins and spots of red. Philip Philipovich plunged his scissors between the membranes and eased them apart. Once a thin stream of blood spurted up, almost hitting the professor in the eye and spattering his white cap. Like a tiger Bormenthal pounced in with a tourniquet and squeezed. Sweat streamed down his face, which was growing puffy and mottled. His eyes flicked to and fro from the professor's hand to the instrument table. Philip Philipovich was positively awe-inspiring. A hoarse snoring noise came from his nose, his teeth were bared to the gums. He peeled aside layers of cerebral membrane and penetrated deep between the hemispheres of the brain. It was then that Bormenthal went pale, and seizing Sharik's breast with one hand he said hoarsely: 'Pulse falling sharply . . .'

Philip Philipovich flashed him a savage look, grunted something and delved further still. Bormenthal snapped open a glass ampoule, filled a syringe with the liquid and treacherously injected the dog near his heart.

'I'm coming to the Turkish saddle,' growled Philip Philipovich. With his slippery, bloodstained gloves he removed Sharik's greyish-yellow brain from his head. For a second he glanced at Sharik's muzzle and Bormenthal snapped open a second ampoule of yellow liquid and sucked it into the long syringe.

'Shall I do it straight into the heart?' he enquired cautiously.

'Don't waste time asking questions!' roared the professor angrily. 'He could die five times over while you're making up your mind. Inject, man! What are you waiting for?' His face had the look of an inspired robber chieftain.

With a flourish the doctor plunged the needle into the dog's heart.

'He's alive, but only just,' he whispered timidly.

'No time to argue whether he's alive or not,' hissed the terrible Philip Philipovich. 'I'm at the saddle. So what if he does die ... hell ... "... the banks of the sa-acred Nile" ... give me the gland.'

Bormenthal handed him a beaker containing a white blob suspended on a thread in some fluid. With one hand ('God, there's no one like him in all Europe,' thought Bormenthal) he fished out the dangling blob and with the other hand, using the scissors, he excised a similar blob from deep within the separated cerebral hemispheres. Sharik's blob he threw on to a plate, the new one he inserted into the brain with a piece of thread. Then his stumpy fingers, now miraculously delicate and sensitive, sewed the amber-coloured thread cunningly into place. After that he removed various stretchers and clamps from the skull, replaced the brain in its bony container, leaned back and said in a much calmer voice: 'I suppose he's died?'

'There's just a flicker of pulse,' replied Bormenthal.

'Give him another shot of adrenalin.'

The professor replaced the membranes over the brain, restored the sawn-off lid to its exact place, pushed the scalp back into position and roared: 'Suture!'

Five minutes later Bormenthal had sewn up the dog's head, breaking three needles.

There on the bloodstained pillow lay Sharik's slack, lifeless muzzle, a circular wound on his tonsured head. Like a satisfied vampire Philip Philipovich finally stepped back, ripped off one glove, shook out of it a cloud of sweat-drenched powder, tore off the other one, threw it on the ground and rang the bell in the wall. Zina appeared in the doorway, looking away to avoid seeing the blood-spattered dog. With chalky hands the great man pulled off his skull-cap and cried:

'Give me a cigarette, Zina. And then some clean clothes and a bath.'

Laying his chin on the edge of the table he parted the dog's right eyelids, peered into the obviously moribund eye and said:

'Well, I'll be ... He's not dead yet. Still, he'll die. I feel sorry for the dog, Bormenthal. He was naughty but I couldn't help liking him.'

Four

Subject of experiment: Male dog aged approx. 2 years.
Breed: Mongrel.
Name: 'Sharik'.

Coat sparse, in tufts, brownish with traces of singeing. Tail the colour of baked milk. On right flank traces of healed second-degree burn. Previous nutritional state— poor. After a week's stay with Prof. Preobrazhensky— extremely well nourished.

Weight: 8 kilograms (!).
Heart: . . .
Lungs: . . .
Stomach: . . .
Temperature: . . .

December 23rd At 8:05 p.m. Prof. Preobrazhensky commenced the first operation of its kind to be performed in Europe: removal under anaesthesia of the dog's testicles and their replacement by implanted human testes, with appendages and seminal ducts, taken from a 28-year-old human male, dead 4 hours and 4 minutes before the operation and kept by Prof. Preobrazhensky in sterilized physiological fluid.

Immediately thereafter, following a trepanning operation on the cranial roof, the pituitary gland was removed and replaced by a human pituitary originating from the above-mentioned human male.

Drugs used: Chloroform—8 cc.

                        Camphor—1 syringe.

                        Adrenalin—2 syringes (by cardiac injection).

Purpose of operation: Experimental observation by Prof. Preobrazhensky of the effect of combined transplantation of the pituitary and testes in order to study both the functional viability in a host-organism and its role in cellular etc. rejuvenation.

Operation performed by: Prof. P. P. Preobrazhensky.
Assisted by: Dr I. A. Bormenthal.

During the night following the operation, frequent and grave weakening of the pulse. Dog apparently in terminal state.

Preobrazhensky prescribes camphor injections in massive dosage.

December 24th a.m. Improvement.
Respiration rate doubled.
Temperature: 42°C.
Camphor and caffeine injected subcutaneously.

December 25th Deterioration.
Pulse barely detectable, cooling of the extremities, no pupillary reaction. Preobrazhensky orders cardiac injection of adrenalin and camphor, intravenous injections of physiological solution.

December 26th Slight improvement.

Pulse: 180.

Respiration: 92.

Temperature: 41°C.

Camphor.

Alimentation per rectum.

December 27th Pulse: 152.

Respiration: 50.

Temperature: 39.8°C.

Pupillary reaction.

Camphor—subcutaneous.

December 28th Significant improvement.

At noon sudden heavy perspiration.

Temperature: 37°C.

Condition of surgical wounds unchanged.

Re-bandaged.

Signs of appetite. Liquid alimentation.

December 29th Sudden moulting of hair on forehead and torso.

The following were summoned for consultation:

1. Professor of Dermatology—Vasily Vasilievich

Bundaryov.

2. Director, Moscow Veterinary Institute.

Both stated the case to be without precedent in medical literature.

No diagnosis established.

Temperature: (entered in pencil).

8:15 p.m. First bark.

Distinct alteration of timbre and lowering of pitch

noticeable. Instead of diphthong 'aow-aow', bark now enunciated on vowels 'ah-oh', in intonation reminiscent of a groan.

December 30th Moulting process has progressed to almost total baldness.

Weighing produced the unexpected result of 30 kg., due to growth (lengthening of the bones). Dog still lying prone.

December 31st Subject exhibits colossal appetite.

(Ink blot. After the blot the following entry in scrawled handwriting): At 12:12 p.m. the dog distinctly pronounced the sounds 'Nes-set-a'.

(Gap in entries. The following entries show errors due to excitement):

December 1st (deleted; corrected to): *January 1st 1925.*

Dog photographed a.m.

Cheerfully barks 'Nes-set-a', repeating loudly and with apparent pleasure.

3:00 p.m. (in heavy lettering): Dog laughed, causing maid Zina to faint. Later, pronounced the following 8 times in succession: 'Nesseta-ciled'.

(Sloping characters, written in pencil):

The professor has deciphered the word 'Nesseta-ciled' by reversal: it is 'delicatessen' ... Quite extraord ...

January 2nd Dog photographed by magnesium flash while smiling. Got up and remained confidently on hind legs for a half-hour. Now nearly my height.

(Loose page inserted into notebook): Russian science almost suffered a most serious blow.

History of Prof P. P. Preobrazhensky's illness:

1:13 p.m. Prof. Preobrazhensky falls into deep faint. On falling, strikes head on edge of table.

Temp.: . . .

The dog in the presence of Zina and myself, had called Prof. Preobrazhensky a 'bloody bastard'.

January 6th (entries made partly in pencil, partly in violet ink): Today, after the dog's tail had fallen out, he quite clearly pronounced the word 'liquor'.

Recording apparatus switched on. God knows what's happening.

(Total confusion.)

Professor has ceased to see patients. From 5:00 p.m. this evening sounds of vulgar abuse issuing from the consulting room, where the creature is still confined. Heard to ask for 'another one, and make it a double.'

January 7th Creature can now pronounce several words: 'taxi', 'full up', 'evening paper', 'take one home for the kiddies' and every known Russian swear word. His appearance is strange. He now has hair only on his head, chin and chest. Elsewhere he is bald, with flabby skin. His genital region now has the appearance of an immature human male. His skull has enlarged considerably. Brow low and receding.

My God, I must be going mad . . .

Philip Philipovich still feels unwell. Most of the observations (pictures and recordings) are being carried out by myself.

Rumours are spreading round the town . . .

Consequences may be incalculable. All day today the whole street was full of loafing rubbernecks and old women . . . Dogs still crowding round beneath the windows. Amazing report in the morning papers: *The rumours of a Martian in Obukhov Street are totally unfounded. They have been spread by black-market traders and their repetition will be severely punished.*

What Martian, for God's sake? This is turning into a nightmare.

Reports in today's evening paper even worse—they say that a child has been born who could play the violin from birth. Beside it is a photograph of myself with the caption: 'Prof. Preobrazhensky performing a Caesarian operation on the mother.' The situation is getting out of hand . . . He can now say a new word—'policeman' . . .

Apparently Darya Petrovna was in love with me and pinched the snapshot of me out of Philip Philipovich's photograph album. After I had kicked out all the reporters one of them sneaked back into the kitchen, and so . . .

Consulting hours are now impossible. Eighty-two telephone calls today. The telephone has been cut off. We are besieged by child-less women . . .

House committee appeared in full strength, headed by Shvonder—they could not explain why they had come.

January 8th Late this evening diagnosis finally agreed. With the impartiality of a true scholar Philip Philipovich has acknowledged his error: transplantation of the pituitary induces not rejuvenation but *total humanization* (underlined three times). This does not, however, lessen the value of his stupendous discovery.

The creature walked round the flat today for the first time. Laughed in the corridor after looking at the electric light. Then, accompanied by Philip Philipovich and myself, he went into the study. Stands firmly on his hind (deleted) . . . his legs and gives the impression of a short, ill-knit human male.

Laughed in the study. His smile is disagreeable and somehow artificial. Then he scratched the back of his head, looked round and registered a further, clearly pronounced word: 'Bourgeois'. Swore. His swearing is methodical, uninterrupted and apparently totally meaningless. There is something mechanical about it—it is as if this creature had heard all this bad language at an earlier phase, automatically recorded it in his subconscious and now regurgitates it wholesale. However, I am no psychiatrist.

The swearing somehow has a very depressing effect on Philip Philipovich. There are moments when he abandons his cool, unemotional observation of new phenomena and appears to lose patience. Once when the creature was swearing, for instance, he suddenly burst out impulsively: 'Shut up!'

This had no effect.

After his visit to the study Sharik was shut up in the consulting room by our joint efforts. Philip Philipovich and I then held a conference. I confess that this was the first time I had seen this self-assured and highly intelligent man at a loss. He hummed a little, as he is in the habit of doing, then asked: 'What are we going to do now?' He answered himself literally as follows: 'Moscow State Clothing Stores, yes . . . "from Granada to Seville" . . . M.S.C.S., my dear doctor . . .' I could not understand him, then he explained: 'Ivan Arnoldovich, please go and buy him some underwear, shirt, jacket and trousers.'

January 9th The creature's vocabulary is being enriched by a new word every five minutes (on average) and, since this morning, by sentences. It is as if they had been lying frozen in his mind, are melting and emerging. Once out, the word remains in use. Since yesterday evening the machine has recorded the following: 'Stop pushing', 'You swine', 'Get off the bus—full up', 'I'll show you', 'American recognition', 'kerosene stove'.

January 10th The creature was dressed. He took to a vest quite readily, even laughing cheerfully. He refused underpants, though, protesting with hoarse shrieks: 'Stop queue-barging, you bastards!' Finally we dressed him. The sizes of his clothes were too big for him.

(Here the notebook contains a number of schematized drawings, apparently depicting the transformation of a canine into a human leg.) The rear half of the skeleton of the foot is lengthening. Elongation of the toes. Nails. (With appropriate sketches.)

Repeated systematic toilet training. The servants are angry and depressed.

However, the creature is undoubtedly intelligent. The experiment is proceeding satisfactorily.

January 11th Quite reconciled to wearing clothes, although was heard to say, 'Christ, I've got ants in my pants.'

Fur on head now thin and silky; almost indistinguishable from hair, though scars still visible in parietal region. Today last traces of fur dropped from his ears. Colossal appetite. Enjoys salted herring. At 5:00 p.m. occurred a significant event: for the first time the words spoken by the creature were not disconnected from surrounding phenomena but were a reaction to them. Thus when the professor said to him, 'Don't throw food scraps on the floor,' he unexpectedly replied: 'Get stuffed.' Philip Philipovich was appalled, but recovered and said: 'If you swear at me or the doctor again, you're in trouble.' I photographed Sharik at that moment and I swear that he understood what the professor said. His face clouded over and he gave a sullen look, but said nothing. Hurrah—he understands!

January 12th. Put hands in pockets. We are teaching him not to swear. Whistled, 'Hey, little apple'. Sustained conversation. I cannot resist certain hypotheses: we must forget rejuvenation for the time being. The other aspect is immeasurably more important. Prof. Preobrazhensky's astounding experiment has revealed one of the secrets of the human brain. The mysterious function of the pituitary as an adjunct to the brain has now been clarified. It determines human appearance. Its hormones may now be regarded as the most important in the whole organism—the hormones of man's image. A new field has been opened up to science; without the aid of any Faustian retorts a homunculus has been created. The surgeon's scalpel has brought to life a new human entity. Prof. Preobrazhensky—you are a creator. (ink blot)

But I digress . . . As stated, he can now sustain a conversation. As I see it, the situation is as follows: the implanted pituitary has activated the speech centre in the canine brain and words have poured out in a stream. I do not think that we have before us a newly created brain but a brain which has been stimulated to develop. Oh, what a glorious confirmation of the theory of evolution! Oh, the sublime chain leading from a dog to Mendeleyev the great chemist! A further hypothesis of mine is that during its canine stage Sharik's brain had accumulated a massive quantity of sense data. All the words which he used initially were the language of the streets which he had picked up and stored in his brain. Now as I walk along the streets I look at every dog I meet with secret horror. God knows what is lurking in their minds.

Sharik can read. He can read (three exclamation marks). I guessed it from his early use of the word 'delicatessen'. He could read from the beginning. And I even know the solution to this puzzle—it lies in the structure of the canine optic nerve. God alone knows what is now going on in Moscow. Seven black-market traders are already behind bars for spreading rumours that the end of the world is imminent and has been caused by the Bolsheviks. Darya Petrovna told me about this and even named the date—November 28th, 1925, the day of St Stephen the Martyr, when the earth will spiral off into infinity . . . Some charlatans are already giving lectures about it. We have started such a rumpus with this pituitary experiment that I have had to leave my flat. I have moved in with Preobrazhensky and sleep in the waiting room with Sharik. The consulting room has been turned into a new waiting room. Shvonder was right. Trouble is brewing with the house committee. There is not a single glass left, as he will jump on to the shelves. Great difficulty in teaching him not to do this.

Something odd is happening to Philip. When I told him about my hypotheses and my hopes of developing Sharik into an intellectually advanced personality, he hummed and hahed, then said: 'Do you really think so?' His tone was ominous. Have I made a mistake? Then he had an idea. While I wrote up these case notes, Preobrazhensky made a careful study of the life story of the man from whom we took the pituitary.

(Loose page inserted into the notebook.)

Name: Klim Grigorievich Chugunkin.
Age: 25.
Marital status: Unmarried.
Not a Party member, but sympathetic to the Party. Three times charged with theft and acquitted—on the first occasion for lack of evidence, in the second case saved by his social origin, the third time put on probation with a conditional sentence of 15 years hard labour.
Profession: plays the balalaika in bars.
Short, poor physical shape.
Enlarged liver (alcohol).
Cause of death: knife-wound in the heart, sustained in the Red Light Bar at Preobrazhensky Gate.

The old man continues to study Chugunkin's case exhaustively, although I cannot understand why. He grunted something about the pathologist having failed to make a complete examination of Chugunkin's body. What does he mean? Does it matter whose pituitary it is?

January 17th Unable to make notes for several days, as I have had an attack of influenza. Meanwhile the creature's appearance has assumed definitive form:

(a) physically a complete human being.
(b) weight about 108 lbs.
(c) below medium height.
(d) small head.
(e) eats human food.
(f) dresses himself.
(g) capable of normal conversation.

So much for the pituitary (ink blot).

This concludes the notes on this case. We now have a new organism which must be studied as such.

Appendices: Verbatim reports of speech, recordings, photographs.
Signed: I. A. Bormenthal, M.D.
Asst. to Prof. P. P. Preobrazhensky.

Five

A winter afternoon in late January, the time before supper, the time before the start of evening consulting hours. On the drawing room doorpost hung a sheet of paper, on which was written in Philip Philipovich's hand:

I forbid the consumption of sunflower seeds in this flat.
P. Preobrazhensky

Below this in big, thick letters Bormenthal had written in blue pencil:

Musical instruments may not be played between 7:00 p.m. and 5:00 a.m.

Then from Zina:

When you come back tell Philip Philipovich that he's gone out and I don't know where to. Fyodor says he's with Shvonder.

Preobrazhensky's hand:

How much longer do I have to wait before the glazier comes?

Darya Petrovna (in block letters):

Zina has gone out to the store, says she'll bring him back.

In the dining room there was a cosy evening feeling, generated by the lamp on the sideboard shining beneath its dark cerise shade. Its light was reflected in random shafts all over the room, as the mirror was cracked from side to side and had been stuck in place with a criss-cross of tape. Bending over the table, Philip Philipovich was absorbed in the large double page of an open newspaper. His face was working with fury and through his teeth issued a jerky stream of abuse. This is what he was reading:

> *There's no doubt that it is his illegitimate (as they used to say in rotten bourgeois society) son. This is how the pseudo-learned members of our bourgeoisie amuse themselves. He will only keep his seven rooms until the glittering sword of justice flashes over him like a red ray. Sh . . . r.*

Someone was hard at work playing a rousing tune on the balalaika two rooms away and the sound of a series of intricate variations on 'The Moon is Shining' mingled in Philip Philipovich's head with the words of the sickening newspaper article. When he had read it he pretended to spit over his shoulder and hummed absentmindedly through his teeth: ' "The moo-oon is shining . . . shining bright . . . the moon is shining . . ." God, that damned tune's on my brain!'

He rang. Zina's face appeared in the doorway.

'Tell him it's five o'clock and he's to shut up. Then tell him to come here, please.'

Philip Philipovich sat down in an armchair beside his desk,

a brown cigar butt between the fingers of his left hand. Leaning against the doorpost there stood, legs crossed, a short man of unpleasant appearance. His hair grew in clumps of bristles like a stubble field and on his face was a meadow of unshaven fluff. His brow was strikingly low. A thick brush of hair began almost immediately above his spreading eyebrows.

His jacket, torn under the left armpit, was covered with bits of straw, his checked trousers had a hole on the right knee and the left leg was stained with violet paint. Round the man's neck was a poisonously bright blue tie with a gilt tie-pin. The colour of the tie was so garish that whenever Philip Philipovich covered his tired eyes and gazed at the complete darkness of the ceiling or the wall, he imagined he saw a flaming torch with a blue halo. As soon as he opened them he was blinded again, dazzled by a pair of patent-leather boots with white spats.

'Like galoshes,' thought Philip Philipovich with disgust. He sighed, sniffed and busied himself with relighting his dead cigar. The man in the doorway stared at the professor with lacklustre eyes and smoked a cigarette, dropping the ash down his shirt front.

The clock on the wall beside a carved wooden grouse struck five o'clock. The inside of the clock was still wheezing as Philip Philipovich spoke.

'I think I have asked you twice not to sleep by the stove in the kitchen—particularly in the daytime.'

The man gave a hoarse cough as though he were choking on a bone and replied:

'It's nicer in the kitchen.'

His voice had an odd quality, at once muffled yet resonant, as if he were far away and talking into a small barrel.

Philip Philipovich shook his head and asked:

'Where on earth did you get that disgusting thing from? I mean your tie.'

Following the direction of the pointing finger, the man's eyes squinted as he gazed lovingly down at his tie.

'What's disgusting about it?' he said. 'It's a very smart tie. Darya Petrovna gave it to me.'

'In that case Darya Petrovna has very poor taste. Those boots are almost as bad. Why did you get such horrible shiny ones? Where did you buy them? What did I tell you? I told you to find yourself a pair of *decent* boots. Just look at them. You don't mean to tell me that Doctor Bormenthal chose them, do you?'

'I told him to get patent-leather ones. Why shouldn't I wear them? Everybody else does. If you go down Kuznetzky Street you'll see nearly everybody wearing patent-leather boots.'

Philip Philipovich shook his head and pronounced weightily:

'No more sleeping in the kitchen. Understand? I've never heard of such behaviour. You're a nuisance there and the women don't like it.'

The man scowled and his lips began to pout.

'So what? Those women act as though they owned the place. They're just maids, but you'd think they were commissars. It's Zina—she's always bellyaching about me.'

Philip Philipovich gave him a stern look.

'Don't you dare talk about Zina in that tone of voice! Understand?'

Silence.

'I'm asking you—do you understand?'

'Yes, I understand.'

'Take that trash off your neck. Sha ... if you saw yourself

in a mirror you'd realize what a fright it makes you look. You look like a clown. For the hundredth time—don't throw cigarette ends on to the floor. And I don't want to hear any more swearing in this flat! And don't spit everywhere! The spittoon's over there. Kindly take better aim when you pee. Cease all further conversation with Zina. She complains that you lurk round her room at night. And don't be rude to my patients! Where do you think you are—in some dive?'

'Don't be so hard on me, Dad,' the man suddenly said in a tearful whine.

Philip Philipovich turned red and his spectacles flashed.

'Who are you calling "Dad"? What impertinent familiarity! I never want to hear that word again! You will address me by my name and patronymic!'

The man flared up impudently: 'Oh, why can't you lay off? Don't spit . . . don't smoke . . . don't go there, don't do this, don't do that . . . sounds like the rules in a tram. Why don't you leave me alone, for God's sake? And why shouldn't I call you "Dad", anyway? I didn't ask you to do the operation, did I?'—the man barked indignantly—'A nice business—you get an animal, slice his head open and now you're sick of him. Perhaps I wouldn't have given permission for the operation. Nor would . . . (the man stared up at the ceiling as though trying to remember a phrase he had been taught) . . . nor would my relatives. I bet I could sue you if I wanted to.'

Philip Philipovich's eyes grew quite round and his cigar fell out of his fingers. 'Well, I'll be . . .' he thought to himself.

'So you object to having been turned into a human being, do you?' he asked, frowning slightly. 'Perhaps you'd prefer to be sniffing around dustbins again? Or freezing in doorways? Well, if I'd known that I wouldn't . . .'

'So what if I had to eat out of dustbins? At least it was

an honest living. And supposing I'd died on your operating table? What d'you say to that, comrade?'

'My name is Philip Philipovich!' exclaimed the professor irritably. 'I'm not your comrade! This is monstrous!' ('I can't stand it much longer,' he thought to himself.)

'Oh, yes!' said the man sarcastically, triumphantly uncrossing his legs. 'I know! Of course we're not comrades! How could we be? I didn't go to college, I don't own a flat with fifteen rooms and a bathroom. Only all that's changed now—now everybody has the right to . . .'

Growing rapidly paler, Philip Philipovich listened to the man's argument. Then the creature stopped and swaggered demonstratively over to an ashtray with a chewed butt-end in his fingers. He spent a long time stubbing it out, with a look on his face which clearly said: 'Drop dead!' Having put out his cigarette he suddenly clicked his teeth and poked his nose under his armpit.

'You're supposed to catch fleas with your *fingers!*' shouted Philip Philipovich in fury. 'Anyhow, how is it that you still have any fleas?'

'You don't think I breed them on purpose, do you?' said the man, offended. 'I suppose fleas just like me, that's all.' With this he poked his fingers through the lining of his jacket, scratched around and produced a tuft of downy red hair.

Philip Philipovich turned his gaze upwards to the plaster rosette on the ceiling and started drumming his fingers on the desk. Having caught his flea, the man sat down in a chair, sticking his thumbs behind the lapels of his jacket. Squinting down at the parquet, he inspected his boots, which gave him great pleasure. Philip Philipovich also looked down at the highlights glinting on the man's blunt-toed boots, frowned and enquired:

'What else were you going to say?'

'Oh, nothing, really. I need some papers, Philip Philipovich.'

Philip Philipovich winced. 'Hm . . . papers, eh? Really, well . . . Hm . . . Perhaps we might . . .' His voice sounded vague and unhappy.

'Now, look,' said the man firmly. 'I can't manage without papers. After all, you know damn well that people who don't have any papers aren't allowed to exist nowadays. To begin with, there's the house committee.'

'What does the house committee have to do with it?'

'A lot. Every time I meet one of them they ask me when I'm going to get registered.'

'Oh, God,' moaned Philip Philipovich. ' "Every time you meet one of them . . ." I can just imagine what you tell them. I thought I told you not to hang about the staircases, anyway.'

'What am I—a convict?' said the man in amazement. His glow of righteous indignation made even his fake ruby tiepin light up. '"Hang about" indeed! That's an insult. I walk about just like everybody else.'

So saying he wriggled his patent-leather feet.

Philip Philipovich said nothing, but looked away. 'One must restrain oneself,' he thought, as he walked over to the sideboard and drank a glassful of water at one gulp.

'I see,' he said rather more calmly. 'All right, I'll overlook your tone of voice for the moment. What does your precious house committee say, then?'

'Hell, I don't know exactly. Anyway, you needn't be sarcastic about the house committee. It protects people's interests.'

'Whose interests, may I ask?'

'The workers', of course.'

Philip Philipovich opened his eyes wide. 'What makes you think that you're a worker?'

'I must be—I'm not a capitalist.'

'Very well. How does the house committee propose to stand up for your revolutionary rights?'

'Easy. Put me on the register. They say they've never heard of anybody being allowed to live in Moscow without being registered. That's for a start. But the most important thing is an identity card. I don't want to be arrested for being a deserter.'

'And where, pray, am I supposed to register you? On that tablecloth or on my own passport? One must, after all, be realistic. Don't forget that you are ... hm, well ... you are what you might call a ... an unnatural phenomenon, an artefact ...' Philip Philipovich sounded less and less convincing.

Triumphant, the man said nothing.

'Very well. Let's assume that in the end we shall have to register you, if only to please this house committee of yours. The trouble is—you have no name.'

'So what? I can easily choose one. Just put it in the newspapers and there you are.'

'What do you propose to call yourself?'

The man straightened his tie and replied: 'Poligraph Poligraphovich.'

'Stop playing the fool,' groaned Philip Philipovich. 'I meant it seriously.'

The man's face twitched sarcastically.

'I don't get it,' he said ingenuously. 'I mustn't swear. I mustn't spit. Yet all you ever do is call me names. I suppose only professors are allowed to swear in the RSFSR.'

Blood rushed to Philip Philipovich's face. He filled a glass, breaking it as he did so. Having drunk from another one, he thought: 'Much more of this, and he'll start teaching me how to behave, and he'll be right. I must control myself.'

He turned round, made an exaggeratedly polite bow and said with iron self-control: 'I beg your pardon. My nerves are slightly upset. Your name struck me as a little odd, that is all. Where, as a matter of interest, did you dig it up?'

'The house committee helped me. We looked in the calendar. And I chose a name.'

'That name cannot possibly exist on any calendar.'

'Can't it?' The man grinned. 'Then how was it I found it on the calendar in your consulting room?'

Without getting up Philip Philipovich leaned over to the knob on the wall and Zina appeared in answer to the bell.

'Bring me the calendar from the consulting room.'

There was a pause. When Zina returned with the calendar, Philip Philipovich asked: 'Where is it?'

'The name day is March 4.'

'Show me . . . hm . . . dammit, throw the thing into the stove at once.' Zina, blinking with fright, removed the calendar. The man shook his head reprovingly.

'And what surname will you take?'

'I'll use my real name.'

'Your *real* name? What is it?'

'Sharikov.'

Shvonder the house committee chairman was standing in his leather tunic in front of the professor's desk. Doctor Bormenthal was seated in an armchair. The doctor's glowing face (he had just come in from the cold) wore an expression whose perplexity was only equalled by that of Philip Philipovich.

'*Write* it?' he asked impatiently.

'Yes,' said Shvonder, 'it's not very difficult. Write a certificate, professor. You know the sort of thing—'This is to certify that the bearer is really Poligraph Poligraphovich Sharikov . . . hm, born in, hm . . . this flat.'

Bormenthal wriggled uneasily in his armchair. Philip Philipovich tugged at his moustache.

'God dammit, I've never heard anything so ridiculous in my life. He wasn't *born* at all, he simply . . . well, he sort of . . .'

'That's your problem,' said Shvonder with quiet malice. 'It's up to you to decide whether he was born or not . . . It was your experiment, professor, and you brought citizen Sharikov into the world.'

'It's all quite simple,' barked Sharikov from the glass-fronted cabinet, where he was admiring the reflection of his tie.

'Kindly keep out of this conversation,' growled Philip Philipovich. 'It's not at all simple.'

'Why shouldn't I join in?' spluttered Sharikov in an offended voice, and Shvonder instantly supported him.

'I'm sorry, professor, but citizen Sharikov is absolutely correct. He has a right to take part in a discussion about his affairs, especially as it's about his identity documents. An identity document is the most important thing in the world.'

At that moment a deafening ring from the telephone cut into the conversation. Philip Philipovich said into the receiver: 'Yes . . .', then reddened and shouted: 'Will you please not distract me with trivialities. What's it to do with you?' And he hurled the receiver back on to the hook.

Delight spread over Shvonder's face.

Purpling, Philip Philipovich roared: 'Right, let's get this finished.'

He tore a sheet of paper from a notepad and scribbled a few words, then read it aloud in a voice of exasperation:

' "I hereby certify ..." God, what am I supposed to certify? ... Let's see ... "That the bearer is a man created during a laboratory experiment by means of an operation on the brain and that he requires identity papers" ... "I object in principle to his having these idiotic documents, but still" ... Signed: "Professor Preobrazhensky!" '

'Really, professor,' said Shvonder in an offended voice. 'What do you mean by calling these documents idiotic? I can't allow an undocumented tenant to go on living in this house, especially one who hasn't been registered with the police for military service. Supposing war suddenly breaks out with the imperialist aggressors?'

'I'm not going to fight!' yapped Sharikov.

Shvonder was dumbfounded, but quickly recovered himself and said politely to Sharikov: 'I'm afraid you seem to be completely lacking in political consciousness, citizen Sharikov. You must register for military service at once.'

'I'll register, but I'm damned if I'm going to fight,' answered Sharikov nonchalantly, straightening his tie.

Now it was Shvonder's turn to be embarrassed. Preobrazhensky exchanged a look of grim complicity with Bormenthal, who nodded meaningly.

'I was badly wounded during the operation,' whined Sharikov. 'Look—they cut me right open.' He pointed to his head. The scar of a fresh surgical wound bisected his forehead.

'Are you an anarchist-individualist?' asked Shvonder, raising his eyebrows.

'I ought to be exempt on medical grounds,' said Sharikov.

'Well, there's no hurry about it,' said the disconcerted Shvonder. 'Meanwhile we'll send the professor's certificate to the police and they'll issue your papers.'

'Er, look here . . .' Philip Philipovich suddenly interrupted him, obviously struck by an idea. 'I suppose you don't have a room to spare in the house, do you? I'd be prepared to buy it.'

Yellowish sparks flashed in Shvonder's brown eyes.

'No, professor, I very much regret to say that we don't have a room. And aren't likely to, either.'

Philip Philipovich clenched his teeth and said nothing. Again the telephone rang as though to order. Without a word Philip Philipovich flicked the receiver off the rest so that it hung down, spinning slightly, on its blue cord. Everybody jumped. 'The old man's getting rattled,' thought Bormenthal. With a glint in his eyes Shvonder bowed and went out.

Sharikov disappeared after him, his boots creaking.

The professor and Bormenthal were left alone. After a short silence, Philip Philipovich shook his head gently and said:

'On my word of honour, this is becoming an absolute nightmare. Don't you see? I swear, doctor, that I've suffered more these last fourteen days than in the past fourteen years! I tell you, he's a scoundrel . . .'

From a distance came the faint tinkle of breaking glass, followed by a stifled woman's scream, then silence. An evil spirit dashed down the corridor, turned into the consulting room, where it produced another crash, and immediately turned back. Doors slammed and Darya Petrovna's low cry was heard from the kitchen. There was a howl from Sharikov.

'Oh, God, what now!' cried Philip Philipovich, rushing for the door.

'A cat,' guessed Bormenthal and leaped after him. They ran down the corridor into the hall, burst in, then turned into the passage leading to the bathroom and the kitchen. Zina came dashing out of the kitchen and ran full tilt into Philip Philipovich.

'How many times have I told you not to let cats into the flat,' shouted Philip Philipovich in fury. 'Where is he? Ivan Arnoldovich, for God's sake go and calm the patients in the waiting room!'

'He's in the bathroom, the devil,' cried Zina, panting. Philip Philipovich hurled himself at the bathroom door, but it would not give way.

'Open up this minute!'

The only answer from the locked bathroom was the sound of something leaping up at the walls, smashing glasses, and Sharikov's voice roaring through the door: 'I'll kill you . . .'

Water could be heard gurgling through the pipes and pouring into the bathtub. Philip Philipovich leaned against the door and tried to break it open. Darya Petrovna, clothes torn and face distorted with anger, appeared in the kitchen doorway. Then the glass transom window, high up in the wall between the bathroom and the kitchen, shattered with a multiple crack. Two large fragments crashed into the kitchen followed by a tabby cat of gigantic proportions with a face like a policeman and a blue bow round its neck. It fell on to the middle of the table, right into a long platter, which it broke in half. From there it fell to the floor, turned round on three legs as it waved the fourth in the air as though executing a dance-step, and instantly streaked out through the back door, which was slightly ajar. The door opened wider and the cat was replaced by the face of an old woman in a headscarf, followed by her polka-dotted skirt. The old woman wiped her mouth with her index and second fingers, stared round the kitchen with protruding eyes that burned with curiosity and said:

'Oh, my lord!'

Pale, Philip Philipovich crossed the kitchen and asked threateningly:

'What do you want?'

'I wanted to have a look at the talking dog,' replied the old woman ingratiatingly and crossed herself. Philip Philipovich went even paler, strode up to her and hissed: 'Get out of my kitchen this instant!'

The old woman tottered back toward the door and said plaintively:

'You needn't be so sharp, professor.'

'Get out, I say!' repeated Philip Philipovich and his eyes went as round as the owl's. He personally slammed the door behind the old woman.

'Darya Petrovna, I've asked you before . . .'

'But Philip Philipovich,' replied Darya Petrovna in desperation, clenching her hands, 'what can I do? People keep coming in all day long, however often I throw them out.'

A dull, threatening roar of water was still coming from the bathroom, although Sharikov was now silent. Doctor Bormenthal came in.

'Please, Ivan Arnoldovich . . . er . . . how many patients are there in the waiting room?'

'Eleven,' replied Bormenthal.

'Send them all away, please. I can't see any patients today.'

With a bony finger Philip Philipovich knocked on the bathroom door and shouted: 'Come out at once! Why have you locked yourself in?'

'Oh . . . oh . . . !' replied Sharikov in tones of misery.

'What on earth . . . I can't hear you—turn off the water.'

'Ow-wow! . . .'

'Turn off the water! What has he done? I don't understand . . .' cried Philip Philipovich, working himself into a frenzy. Zina and Darya Petrovna opened the kitchen door and peeped out. Once again Philip Philipovich thundered on the bathroom door with his fist.

'There he is!' screamed Darya Petrovna from the kitchen. Philip Philipovich rushed in. The distorted features of Poligraph Poligraphovich appeared through the broken transom and leaned out into the kitchen. His eyes were tearstained and there was a long scratch down his nose, red with fresh blood.

'Have you gone out of your mind?' asked Philip Philipovich. 'Why don't you come out of there?'

Terrified and miserable, Sharikov stared around and replied:

'I've shut myself in.'

'Unlock the door, then. Haven't you ever seen a lock before?'

'The blasted thing won't open!' replied Poligraph, terrified.

'Oh, my God, he's shut the safety-catch too!' screamed Zina, wringing her hands.

'There's a sort of button on the lock,' shouted Philip Philipovich, trying to out-roar the water. 'Press it downwards … press it down! Downwards!'

Sharikov vanished, to reappear over the transom a minute later.

'I can't see a thing!' he barked in terror.

'Well, turn the light on then! He's gone crazy!'

'That damned cat smashed the bulb,' replied Sharikov, 'and when I tried to catch the bastard by the leg I turned on the tap and now I can't find it.'

Appalled, all three wrung their hands in horror.

Five minutes later Bormenthal, Zina and Darya Petrovna were sitting in a row on a damp carpet that had been rolled up against the foot of the bathroom door, pressing it hard with their bottoms. Fyodor the porter was climbing up a ladder into the transom window, with the lighted candle from Darya Petrovna's ikon in his hand. His posterior, clad in broad grey checks, hovered in the air, then vanished through the opening.

'Ooh! . . . ow!' came Sharikov's strangled shriek above the roar of water.

Fyodor's voice was heard: 'There's nothing for it, Philip Philipovich, we'll have to open the door and let the water out. We can mop it up from the kitchen.'

'Open it then!' shouted Philip Philipovich angrily.

The three got up from the carpet and pushed the bathroom door open. Immediately a tidal wave gushed out into the passage, where it divided into three streams—one straight into the lavatory opposite, one to the right into the kitchen and one to the left into the hall. Splashing and prancing, Zina shut the door into the hall. Fyodor emerged, up to his ankles in water, and for some reason grinning. He was soaking wet and looked as if he were wearing oilskins.

'The water-pressure was so strong, I only just managed to turn it off,' he explained.

'Where is he?' asked Philip Philipovich, cursing as he lifted one wet foot.

'He's afraid to come out,' said Fyodor, giggling stupidly.

'Will you beat me, Dad?' came Sharikov's tearful voice from the bathroom.

'You idiot!' was Philip Philipovich's terse reply.

Zina and Darya Petrovna, with bare legs and skirts tucked up to their knees, and Sharikov and the porter barefoot with rolled-up trousers were hard at work mopping up the kitchen floor with wet cloths, squeezing them out into dirty buckets and into the sink. The abandoned stove roared away. The water swirled out of the back door, down the well of the back staircase and into the cellar.

On tiptoe, Bormenthal was standing in a deep puddle on the parquet floor of the hall and talking through the crack of the front door, opened only as far as the chain would allow.

'No consulting hours today, I'm afraid, the professor's not well. Please keep away from the door, we have a burst pipe . . .'

'But when can the professor see me?' a voice came through the door. 'It wouldn't take a minute . . .'

'I'm sorry.' Bormenthal rocked back from his toes to his heels. 'The professor's in bed and a pipe has burst. Come tomorrow. Zina dear, quickly mop up the hall or it will start running down the front staircase.'

'There's too much—the cloths won't do it.'

'Never mind,' said Fyodor. 'We'll scoop it up with jugs.'

While the doorbell rang ceaselessly, Bormenthal stood up to his ankles in water.

'When is the operation?' said an insistent voice as it tried to force its way through the crack of the door.

'A pipe's burst . . .'

'But I've come in galoshes . . .'

Bluish silhouettes appeared outside the door.

'I'm sorry, it's impossible, please come tomorrow.'

'But I have an appointment.'

'Tomorrow. There's been a disaster in the water supply.'

Fyodor splashed about in the lake, scooping it up with a jug, but the battle-scared Sharikov had thought up a new method. He rolled up an enormous cloth, lay on his stomach in the water and pushed it backwards from the hall towards the lavatory.

'What d'you think you're doing, you fool, slopping it all round the flat?' fumed Darya Petrovna. 'Pour it into the sink.'

'How can I?' replied Sharikov, scooping up the murky water with his hands. 'If I don't push it back into the flat it'll run out of the front door.'

A bench was pushed creaking out of the corridor, with Philip Philipovich riding unsteadily on it in his blue striped socks.

'Stop answering the door, Ivan Arnoldovich. Go into the bedroom, you can borrow a pair of my slippers.'

'Don't bother, Philip Philipovich, I'm all right.'

'You're wearing nothing but a pair of galoshes.'

'I don't mind. My feet are wet anyway.'

'Oh, my God!' Philip Philipovich was exhausted and depressed.

'Destructive animal!' Sharikov suddenly burst out as he squatted on the floor, clutching a soup tureen.

Bormenthal slammed the door, unable to contain himself any longer and burst into laughter. Philip Philipovich blew out his nostrils and his spectacles glittered.

'What are you talking about?' he asked Sharikov from the eminence of his bench.

'I was talking about the cat. Filthy swine,' answered Sharikov, his eyes swivelling guiltily.

'Look here, Sharikov,' retorted Philip Philipovich, taking a deep breath. 'I swear I have never seen a more impudent creature than you.'

Bormenthal giggled.

'You,' went on Philip Philipovich, 'are nothing but a lout. How dare you say that? You caused the whole thing and you have the gall . . . No, really! It's too much!'

'Tell me, Sharikov,' said Bormenthal, 'how much longer

are you going to chase cats? You ought to be ashamed of yourself. It's disgraceful! You're a savage!'

'Me—a savage?' snarled Sharikov. 'I'm no savage. I won't stand for that cat in this flat. It only comes here to find what it can pinch. It stole Darya's mincemeat. I wanted to teach it a lesson.'

'You should teach yourself a lesson!' replied Philip Philipovich. 'Just take a look at your face in the mirror.'

'Nearly scratched my eyes out,' said Sharikov gloomily, wiping a dirty hand across his eyes.

By the time that the water-blackened parquet had dried out a little, all the mirrors were covered in a veil of condensed vapour and the doorbell had stopped ringing. Philip Philipovich in red morocco slippers was standing in the hall.

'There you are, Fyodor. Thank you.'

'Thank you very much, sir.'

'Mind you change your clothes straight away. No, wait— have a glass of Darya Petrovna's vodka before you go.'

'Thank you, sir,' Fyodor squirmed awkwardly, then said: 'There is one more thing, Philip Philipovich. I'm sorry, I hardly like to mention it, but it's the matter of the window-pane in No 7. Citizen Sharikov threw some stones at it, you see . . .'

'Did he throw them at a cat?' asked Philip Philipovich, frowning like a thundercloud.

'Well, no, he was throwing them at the owner of the flat. He's threatening to sue.'

'Oh, lord!'

'Sharikov tried to kiss their cook and they threw him out. They had a bit of a fight, it seems.'

'For God's sake, do you have to tell me all these disasters at once? How much?'

'One rouble and fifty kopecks.'

Philip Philipovich took out three shining fifty-kopeck pieces and handed them to Fyodor.

'And on top of it all you have to pay one rouble and fifty kopecks because of that damned cat,' grumbled a voice from the doorway. 'It was all the cat's fault . . .'

Philip Philipovich turned round, bit his lip and gripped Sharikov. Without a word he pushed him into the waiting room and locked the door. Sharik immediately started to hammer on the door with his fists.

'Shut up!' shouted Philip Philipovich in a voice that was nearly deranged.

'This is the limit,' said Fyodor meaningfully. 'I've never seen such impudence in my life.'

Bormenthal seemed to materialize out of the floor.

'Please, Philip Philipovich, don't upset yourself.'

The doctor thrust open the door into the waiting room. He could be heard saying: 'Where d'you think you are? In some dive?'

'That's it,' said Fyodor approvingly. 'Serve him right . . . a punch on the ear's what he needs . . .'

'No, not that, Fyodor,' growled Philip Philipovich sadly.

'I think you've just about had all you can take, Philip Philipovich.'

Six

'No, no, no!' insisted Bormenthal. 'You must tuck in your napkin.'

'Why the hell should I,' grumbled Sharikov.

'Thank you, doctor,' said Philip Philipovich gratefully. 'I simply haven't the energy to reprimand him any longer.'

'I shan't allow you to start eating until you put on your napkin. Zina, take the mayonnaise away from Sharikov.'

'Hey, don't do that,' said Sharikov plaintively. 'I'll put it on straight away.'

Pushing away the dish from Zina with his left hand and stuffing a napkin down his collar with the right hand, he looked exactly like a customer in a barber's shop.

'And eat with your fork, please,' added Bormenthal.

Sighing long and heavily Sharikov chased slices of sturgeon around in a thick sauce.

'Can't I have some vodka?' he asked.

'Will you kindly keep quiet?' said Bormenthal. 'You've been at the vodka too often lately.'

'Do you grudge me it?' asked Sharikov, glowering sullenly across the table.

'Stop talking such damn nonsense . . .' Philip Philipovich broke in harshly, but Bormenthal interrupted him.

'Don't worry, Philip Philipovich, leave it to me. You, Sharikov are talking nonsense and the most disturbing thing of all is that you talk it with such complete confidence. Of course I don't grudge you the vodka, especially as it's not mine but belongs to Philip Philipovich. It's simply that it's harmful. That's for a start; secondly you behave badly enough without vodka.' Bormenthal pointed to where the sideboard had been broken and glued together.

'Zina, dear, give me a little more fish please,' said the professor.

Meanwhile Sharikov had stretched out his hand towards the decanter and, with a sideways glance at Bormenthal, poured himself out a glassful.

'You should offer it to the others first,' said Bormenthal. 'Like this—first to Philip Philipovich, then to me, then yourself.'

A faint, sarcastic grin flickered across Sharikov's mouth and he poured out glasses of vodka all round.

'You act just as if you were on parade here,' he said. 'Put your napkin here, your tie there, "please", "thank you", "excuse me"—why can't you behave naturally? Honestly, you stuffed shirts act as if it was still the days of tsarism.'

'What do you mean by "behave naturally"?'

Sharikov did not answer Philip Philipovich's question, but raised his glass and said: 'Here's how . . .'

'And you too,' echoed Bormenthal with a tinge of irony.

Sharikov tossed the glassful down his throat, blinked, lifted a piece of bread to his nose, sniffed it, then swallowed it as his eyes filled with tears.

'Phase,' Philip Philipovich suddenly blurted out, as if preoccupied.

Bormenthal gave him an astonished look. 'I'm sorry? . . .'

'It's a phase,' repeated Philip Philipovich and nodded bitterly. 'There's nothing we can do about it. Klim.'

Deeply interested, Bormenthal glanced sharply into Philip Philipovich's eyes: 'Do you suppose so, Philip Philipovich?'

'I don't suppose; I'm convinced.'

'Can it be that . . .' began Bormenthal, then stopped after a glance at Sharikov, who was frowning suspiciously.

'*Später* . . .' said Philip Philipovich softly.

'*Gut*,' replied his assistant.

Zina brought in the turkey. Bormenthal poured out some red wine for Philip Philipovich, then offered some to Sharikov.

'Not for me, I prefer vodka.' His face had grown puffy, sweat was breaking out on his forehead and he was distinctly merrier. Philip Philipovich also cheered up slightly after drinking some wine. His eyes grew clearer and he looked rather more approvingly at Sharikov, whose black head above his white napkin now shone like a fly in a pool of cream.

Bormenthal however, when fortified, seemed to want activity.

'Well now, what are you and I going to do this evening?' he asked Sharikov.

Sharikov winked and replied: 'Let's go to the circus. I like that best.'

'Why go to the circus every day?' remarked Philip Philipovich in a good-humoured voice. 'It sounds so boring to me. If I were you I'd go to the theatre.'

'I won't go to the theatre,' answered Sharikov nonchalantly and made the sign of the cross over his mouth.

'Hiccuping at table takes other people's appetites away,' said Bormenthal automatically. 'If you don't mind my mentioning it . . . Incidentally, why don't you like the theatre?'

Sharikov held his empty glass up to his eye and looked through it as though it were an opera glass. After some thought he pouted and said:

'Hell, it's just rot . . . talk, talk. Pure counter-revolution.'

Philip Philipovich leaned against his high, carved gothic chairback and laughed so hard that he displayed what looked like two rows of gold fence posts. Bormenthal merely shook his head.

'You should do some reading,' he suggested, 'and then, perhaps . . .'

'But I read a lot . . .' answered Sharikov, quickly and surreptitiously pouring himself half a glass of vodka.

'Zina!' cried Philip Philipovich anxiously. 'Clear away the vodka, my dear. We don't need it any more . . . What have you been reading?'

He suddenly had a mental picture of a desert island, palm trees, and a man dressed in goatskins. 'I'll bet he says *Robinson Crusoe* . . .' he thought.

'That guy . . . what's his name . . . Engels' correspondence with . . . hell, what d'you call him . . . oh—Kautsky.'

Bormenthal's forkful of turkey meat stopped in mid-air and Philip Philipovich choked on his wine. Sharikov seized this moment to gulp down his vodka.

Philip Philipovich put his elbows on the table, stared at Sharikov and asked:

'What comment can you make on what you've read?'

Sharikov shrugged. 'I don't agree.'

'With whom—Engels or Kautsky?'

'With neither of 'em,' replied Sharikov.

'That is most remarkable. Anybody who says that . . . Well, what would you suggest instead?'

'Suggest? I dunno . . . They just write and write all that rot . . . all about some congress and some Germans . . . makes my head reel. Take everything away from the bosses, then divide it up . . .'

'Just as I thought,' exclaimed Philip Philipovich, slapping the tablecloth with his palm. 'Just as I thought.'

'And how is this to be done?' asked Bormenthal with interest.

'How to do it?' Sharikov, grown loquacious with wine, explained garrulously:

'Easy. Fr'instance—here's one guy with seven rooms and forty pairs of trousers and there's another guy who has to eat out of dustbins.'

'I suppose that remark about the seven rooms is a hint about me?' asked Philip Philipovich with a haughty raise of the eyebrows.

Sharikov hunched his shoulders and said no more.

'All right, I've nothing against fair shares. How many patients did you turn away yesterday, doctor?'

'Thirty-nine,' was Bormenthal's immediate reply.

'Hm ... three hundred and ninety roubles, shared between us three. I won't count Zina and Darya Petrovna. Right, Sharikov—that means your share is one hundred and thirty roubles. Kindly hand it over.'

'Hey, wait a minute,' said Sharikov, beginning to be scared. 'What's the idea? What d'you mean?'

'I mean the cat and the tap,' Philip Philipovich suddenly roared, dropping his mask of ironic imperturbability.

'Philip Philipovich!' exclaimed Bormenthal anxiously.

'Don't interrupt. The scene you created yesterday was intolerable, and thanks to you I had to turn away all my patients. You were leaping around in the bathroom like a savage, smashing everything and jamming the taps. Who killed Madame Polasukher's cat? Who ...'

'The day before yesterday, Sharikov, you bit a lady you met on the staircase,' put in Bormenthal.

'You ought to be ...' roared Philip Philipovich.

'But she slapped me across the mouth,' whined Sharikov 'She can't go doing that to me!'

'She slapped you because you pinched her on the bosom,' shouted Bormenthal, knocking over a glass. 'You stand there and ...'

'You belong to the lowest possible stage of development,' Philip Philipovich shouted him down. 'You are still in the formative stage. You are intellectually weak, all your actions are purely bestial. Yet you allow yourself in the presence of two university-educated men to offer advice, with quite intolerable familiarity, on a cosmic scale and of quite cosmic stupidity, on the redistribution of wealth ... and at the same time you eat toothpaste ...'

'The day before yesterday,' added Bormenthal.

'And now,' thundered Philip Philipovich, 'that you have nearly got your nose scratched off—incidentally, why have you wiped the zinc ointment off it?—you can just shut up and listen to what you're told. You are going to learn to behave and try to become a marginally acceptable member of society. By the way, who was fool enough to lend you that book?'

'There you go again—calling everybody fools,' replied Sharikov nervously, deafened by the attack on him from both sides.

'Let me guess,' exclaimed Philip Philipovich, turning red with fury.

'Well, Shvonder gave it to me ... so what? He's not a fool ... it was so I could get educated.'

'I can see which way your education is going after reading Kautsky,' shouted Philip Philipovich, hoarse and turning faintly yellow. With this he gave the bell a furious jab. 'Today's incident shows it better than anything else. Zina!'

'Zina!' shouted Bormenthal.

'Zina!' cried the terrified Sharikov.

Looking pale, Zina ran into the room.

'Zina, there's a book in the waiting room ... It is in the waiting room, isn't it?'

'Yes, it is,' said Sharikov obediently. 'Green, the colour of copper sulphate.'

'A green book ...'

'Burn it if you like,' cried Sharikov in desperation. 'It's only a public library book.'

'It's called *Correspondence* ... *between*, er, Engels and that other man, what's his name ... Anyway, throw it into the stove!'

Zina flew out.

'I'd like to hang that Shvonder, on my word of honour, on the first tree,' said Philip Philipovich, with a furious lunge at a turkey wing. 'There's a gang of poisonous people in this house—it's just like an abscess. To say nothing of his idiotic newspapers ...'

Sharikov gave the professor a look of malicious sarcasm. Philip Philipovich in his turn shot him a sideways glance and said no more.

'Oh, dear, it looks as if nothing's going to go right,' came Bormenthal's sudden and prophetic thought.

Zina brought in a layer cake on a dish and a coffee pot.

'I'm not eating any of that,' Sharikov growled threateningly.

'No one has offered you any. Behave yourself. Please have some, doctor.'

Dinner ended in silence.

Sharikov pulled a crumpled cigarette out of his pocket and lit it. Having drunk his coffee, Philip Philipovich looked at the clock. He pressed his repeater and it gently struck a quarter past eight. As was his habit Philip Philipovich leaned against his gothic chairback and turned to the newspaper on a side table.

'Would you like to go to the circus with him tonight, doctor? Only do check the programme in advance and make sure there are no cats in it.'

'I don't know how they let such filthy beasts into the circus at all,' said Sharikov sullenly, shaking his head.

'Well never mind what filthy beasts they let into the circus for the moment,' said Philip Philipovich ambiguously. 'What's on tonight?'

'At Solomon's,' Bormenthal began to read out, 'there's something called the *Four . . . the Four Yooshems and the Human Ball-Bearing.*'

'What are Yooshems?' enquired Philip Philipovich suspiciously.

'God knows. First time I've ever come across the word.'

'Well in that case you'd better look at Nikita's. We must be absolutely sure about what we're going to see.'

'Nikita's . . . Nikita's . . . hm . . . elephants and the *Ultimate in Human Dexterity.*'

'I see. What is your attitude to elephants, my dear Sharikov?' enquired Philip Philipovich mistrustfully. Sharikov was immediately offended.

'Hell—I don't know. Cats are a special case. Elephants are useful animals,' replied Sharikov.

'Excellent. As long as you think they're useful you can go and watch them. Do as Ivan Arnoldovich tells you. And don't get talking to anyone in the bar! I beg you, Ivan Arnoldovich, not to offer Sharikov beer to drink.'

Ten minutes later Ivan Arnoldovich and Sharikov, dressed

in a peaked cap and a raglan overcoat with turned-up collar, set off for the circus. Silence descended on the flat. Philip Philipovich went into his study. He switched on the lamp under its heavy green shade, which gave the study a great sense of calm, and began to pace the room. The tip of his cigar glowed long and hard with its pale green fire. The professor put his hands into his pockets and deep thoughts racked his balding, learned brow. Now and again he smacked his lips, hummed 'to the banks of the sacred Nile . . .' and muttered something. Finally he put his cigar into the ashtray, went over to the glass cabinet and lit up the entire study with the three powerful lamps in the ceiling. From the third glass shelf Philip Philipovich took out a narrow jar and began, frowning, to examine it by the lamplight. Suspended in a transparent, viscous liquid there swam a little white blob that had been extracted from the depths of Sharik's brain. With a shrug of his shoulders, twisting his lips and murmuring to himself, Philip Philipovich devoured it with his eyes as though the floating white blob might unravel the secret of the curious events which had turned life upside down in that flat on Prechistenka.

It could be that this most learned man did succeed in divining the secret. At any rate, having gazed his full at this cerebral appendage he returned the jar to the cabinet, locked it, put the key into his waistcoat pocket and collapsed, head pressed down between his shoulders and hands thrust deep into his jacket pockets, on to the leather-covered couch. He puffed long and hard at another cigar, chewing its end to fragments. Finally, looking like a greying Faust in the green-tinged lamplight, he exclaimed aloud:

'Yes, by God, I will.'

There was no one to reply. Every sound in the flat was

hushed. By eleven o'clock the traffic in Obukhov Street always died down. The rare footfall of a belated walker echoed in the distance, ringing out somewhere beyond the lowered blinds, then dying away. In Philip Philipovich's study his repeater chimed gently beneath his fingers in his waistcoat pocket ... Impatiently the professor waited for Doctor Bormenthal and Sharikov to return from the circus.

Seven

We do not know what Philip Philipovich had decided to do. He did nothing in particular during the subsequent week and perhaps as a result of this things began happening fast.

About six days after the affair with the bath-water and the cat, the young person from the house committee who had turned out to be a woman came to Sharikov and handed him some papers. Sharikov put them into his pocket and immediately called Doctor Bormenthal.

'Bormenthal!'

'Kindly address me by my name and patronymic!' retorted Bormenthal, his expression clouding. I should mention that in the past six days the great surgeon had managed to quarrel eight times with his ward Sharikov and the atmosphere in the flat was tense.

'All right, then you can call me by *my* name and patronymic too!' replied Sharikov with complete justification.

'No!' thundered Philip Philipovich from the doorway. 'I forbid you to utter such an idiotic name in my flat. If you want us to stop calling you Sharikov, Doctor Bormenthal and I will call you "Mister Sharikov".'

'I'm not mister—all the "misters" are in Paris!' barked Sharikov.

'I see Shvonder's been at work on you!' shouted Philip

Philipovich. 'Well, I'll fix that rascal. There will only be "misters" in my flat as long as I'm living in it! Otherwise either I or you will get out, and it's more likely to be you. I'm putting a "room wanted" advertisement in the papers today and believe me I intend to find you a room.'

'You don't think I'm such a fool as to leave here, do you!' was Sharikov's crisp retort.

'What?' cried Philip Philipovich. Such a change came over his expression that Bormenthal rushed anxiously to his side and gently took him by the sleeve.

'Don't you be so impertinent, Monsieur Sharikov!' said Bormenthal, raising his voice. Sharikov stepped back and pulled three pieces of paper out of his pocket—one green, one yellow and one white, and said as he tapped them with his fingers:

'There. I'm now a member of this residential association and the tenant in charge of flat No. 5, Preobrazhensky, has got to give me my entitlement of thirty-seven square feet . . .' Sharikov thought for a moment and then added a word which Bormenthal's mind automatically recorded as new—'please'.

Philip Philipovich bit his lip and said rashly:

'I swear I'll shoot that Shvonder one of these days.'

It was obvious from the look in Sharikov's eyes that he had taken careful note of the remark.

'*Vorsicht*, Philip Philipovich . . .' warned Bormenthal.

'Well, what do you expect? The gall of it . . . !' shouted Philip Philipovich in Russian.

'Look here, Sharikov . . . *Mister* Sharikov . . . If you commit one more piece of impudence I shall deprive you of your dinner, in fact of all your food. Thirty-seven square feet may be all very well, but there's nothing on that stinking little bit of paper which says that I have to feed you!'

Frightened, Sharikov opened his mouth.

'I can't go without food,' he mumbled. 'Where would I eat?'

'Then behave yourself!' cried both doctors in chorus.

Sharikov relapsed into meaningful silence and did no harm to anybody that day with the exception of himself— taking advantage of Bormenthal's brief absence he got hold of the doctor's razor and cut his cheek-bone so badly that Philip Philipovich and Doctor Bormenthal had to bandage the cut with much wailing and weeping on Sharikov's part.

Next evening two men sat in the green twilight of the professor's study—Philip Philipovich and the faithful, devoted Bormenthal. The house was asleep. Philip Philipovich was wearing his sky-blue dressing gown and red slippers, while Bormenthal was in his shirt and blue braces. On the round table between the doctors, beside a thick album, stood a bottle of brandy, a plate of sliced lemon and a box of cigars. Through the smoke-laden air the two scientists were heatedly discussing the latest event: that evening Sharikov had stolen two ten-rouble notes which had been lying under a paperweight in Philip Philipovich's study, had disappeared from the flat and then returned later completely drunk. But that was not all. With him had come two unknown characters who had created a great deal of noise on the front staircase and expressed a desire to spend the night with Sharikov. The individuals in question were only removed after Fyodor, appearing on the scene with a coat thrown over his underwear, had telephoned the 45th Precinct police station. The individuals vanished instantly as soon as Fyodor had replaced the receiver. After they had gone it was found that a malachite ashtray had mysteriously vanished from a console in the hall, also Philip Philipovich's beaver hat and his walking-stick with a gold band inscribed: 'From the grateful hospital staff to Philip Philipovich in memory of "X"-day with affection and respect.'

'Who were they?' said Philip Philipovich aggressively, clenching his fists. Staggering and clutching the fur-coats, Sharikov muttered something about not knowing who they were, that they were a couple of bastards but good chaps.

'The strangest thing of all was that they were both drunk ... How did they manage to lay their hands on the stuff?' said Philip Philipovich in astonishment, glancing at the place where his presentation walking-stick had stood until recently.

'They're experts,' explained Fyodor as he returned home to bed with a rouble in his pocket.

Sharikov categorically denied having stolen the twenty roubles, mumbling something indistinct about himself not being the only person in the flat.

'Aha, I see—I suppose Doctor Bormenthal stole the money?' enquired Philip Philipovich in a voice that was quiet but terrifying in its intonation.

Sharikov staggered, opened his bleary eyes and offered the suggestion:

'Maybe Zina took it ...'

'What?' screamed Zina, appearing in the doorway like a spectre, clutching an unbuttoned cardigan across her bosom. 'How could he ...'

Philip Philipovich's neck flushed red.

'Calm down, Zina,' he said, stretching out his arm to her, 'don't get upset, we'll fix this.'

Zina immediately burst into tears, her mouth fell wide open and her hand dropped from her bosom.

'Zina—aren't you ashamed? Who could imagine you

taking it? What a disgraceful exhibition!' said Bormenthal in deep embarrassment.

'You silly girl, Zina, God forgive you . . .' began Philip Philipovich.

But at that moment Zina stopped crying and the others froze in horror—Sharikov was feeling unwell. Banging his head against the wall, he was emitting a moan that was pitched somewhere between the vowels 'i' and 'o'—a sort of 'eeuuhh'. His face turned pale and his jaw twitched convulsively.

'Look out—get the swine that bucket from the consulting room!'

Everybody rushed to help the ailing Sharikov. As he staggered off to bed supported by Bormenthal he swore gently and melodiously, despite a certain difficulty in enunciation.

The whole affair had occurred around one a.m. and now it was three a.m., but the two men in the study talked on, fortified by brandy and lemon. The tobacco smoke in the room was so dense that it moved about in slow, flat, unruffled swathes.

Doctor Bormenthal, pale but determined, raised his thin-stemmed glass.

'Philip Philipovich,' he exclaimed with great feeling, 'I shall never forget how as a half-starved student I came to you and you took me under your wing. Believe me, Philip Philipovich, you are much more to me than a professor, a teacher . . . My respect for you is boundless . . . Allow me to embrace you, dear Philip Philipovich . . .'

'Yes, yes, my dear fellow . . .' grunted Philip Philipovich in embarrassment and rose to meet him. Bormenthal embraced him and kissed him on his bushy, nicotine-stained moustaches.

'Honestly, Philip Phili . . .'

'Very touching, very touching . . . Thank you,' said Philip Philipovich. 'I'm afraid I sometimes bawl at you during operations. You must forgive an old man's testiness. The fact is I'm really so lonely . . . ". . . from Granada to Seville . . ." '

'How can you say that, Philip Philipovich?' exclaimed Bormenthal with great sincerity. 'Kindly don't talk like that again unless you want to offend me . . .'

'Thank you, thank you . . . ". . . to the banks of the sacred Nile . . ." . . . thank you . . . I liked you because you were such a competent doctor.'

'I tell you, Philip Philipovich, it's the only way . . .' cried Bormenthal passionately. Leaping up from his place he firmly shut the door leading into the corridor, came back and went on in a whisper: 'Don't you see, it's the only way out? Naturally I wouldn't dare to offer you advice, but look at yourself, Philip Philipovich—you're completely worn out, you're in no fit state to go on working!'

'You're quite right,' agreed Philip Philipovich with a sigh.

'Very well, then, you agree this can't go on,' whispered Bormenthal.

'Last time you said you were afraid for me and I wish you knew, my dear professor, how that touched me. But I'm not a child either and I can see only too well what a terrible affair this could be. But I am deeply convinced that there is no other solution.'

Philip Philipovich stood up, waved his arms at him and cried:

'Don't tempt me. Don't even mention it.' The professor walked up and down the room, disturbing the grey swathes. 'I won't hear of it. Don't you realize what would happen if they found us out? Because of our "social origins" you and I would never get away with it, despite the fact of it being our first offence. I don't suppose your "origins" are any better than mine, are they?'

'I suppose not. My father was a plain-clothes policeman in Vilno,' said Bormenthal as he drained his brandy glass.

'There you are, just as I thought. From the Bolshevik's point of view you couldn't have come from a more unsuitable background. Still, mine is even worse. My father was dean of a cathedral. Perfect. ". . . from Granada to Seville . . . in the silent shades of night . . ." So there we are.'

'But Philip Philipovich, you're a celebrity, a figure of world-wide importance, and just because of some, forgive the expression, bastard . . . Surely they can't touch you!'

'All the same, I refuse to do it,' said Philip Philipovich thoughtfully.

He stopped and stared at the glass-fronted cabinet.

'But why?'

'Because *you* are not a figure of world importance.'

'But what . . .'

'Come now, you don't think I could let you take the rap while I shelter behind my world-wide reputation, do you? Really . . . I'm a Moscow University graduate, not a Sharikov.'

Philip Philipovich proudly squared his shoulders and looked like an ancient king of France.

'Well, then, Philip Philipovich,' sighed Bormenthal. 'What's to be done? Are you just going to wait until that hooligan turns into a human being?'

Philip Philipovich stopped him with a gesture, poured himself a brandy, sipped it, sucked a slice of lemon and said:

'Ivan Arnoldovich. Do you think I understand a little about the anatomy and physiology of, shall we say, the human brain? What's your opinion?'

'Philip Philipovich—what a question!' replied Bormenthal with deep feeling and spread his hands.

'Very well. No need, therefore, for any false modesty. I also believe that I am perhaps not entirely unknown in this field in Moscow.'

'I believe there's no one to touch you, not only in Moscow but in London and Oxford too!' Bormenthal interrupted furiously.

'Good. So be it. Now listen to me, professor-to-be Bormenthal: no one could ever pull it off. It's obvious. No need to ask. If anybody asks you, tell them that Preobrazhensky said so. Finito. Klim!'—Philip Philipovich suddenly cried triumphantly and the glass cabinet vibrated in response. 'Klim,' he repeated. 'Now, Bormenthal, you are the first pupil of my school and apart from that my friend, as I was able to convince myself today. So I will tell you as a friend, in secret—because of course I know that you wouldn't expose me—that this old ass Preobrazhensky bungled that operation like a third-year medical student. It's true that it resulted in a discovery—and you know yourself just what sort of a discovery that was'—here Philip Philipovich pointed sadly with both hands towards the window-blind, obviously pointing to Moscow—'but just remember, Ivan Arnoldovich, that the sole result of that discovery will be that from now on we shall all have that creature Sharik hanging round our necks'— here Preobrazhensky slapped himself on his bent and slightly sclerotic neck—'of that you may be sure! If someone,' went on Philip Philipovich with relish, 'were to knock me down and skewer me right now, I'd give him fifty roubles reward! "... from Granada to Seville ..." ... Dammit, I spent five years doing nothing but extracting cerebral appendages ... You know how much work I did on the subject—an unbelievable amount. And now comes the crucial question—what for? So that one fine day a nice little dog could be transformed into a specimen of so-called humanity so revolting that he makes one's hair stand on end.'

'Well, at least it is a unique achievement.'

'I quite agree with you. This, doctor, is what happens when a researcher, instead of keeping in step with nature, tries to force the pace and lift the veil. Result—Sharikov. We have made our bed and now we must lie on it.'

'Supposing the brain had been Spinoza's, Philip Philipovich?'

'Yes!' bellowed Philip Philipovich. 'Yes! Provided the wretched dog didn't die under the knife—and you saw how tricky the operation was. In short—I, Philip Preobrazhensky would perform the most difficult feat of my whole career by transplanting Spinoza's, or anyone else's pituitary and turning a dog into a highly intelligent being. But what in heaven's name for? That's the point. Will you kindly tell me why one has to manufacture artificial Spinozas when some peasant woman may produce a real one any day of the week? After all, the great Lomonosov was the son of a peasant woman from Kholmogory. Mankind, doctor, takes care of that. Every year evolution ruthlessly casts aside the mass of dross and creates a few dozen men of genius who become an ornament to the whole world. Now I hope you understand why I condemned the deductions you made from Sharikov's case history. My discovery, which you are so concerned about, is worth about as much as a bent penny . . . No, don't argue, Ivan Arnoldovich, I have given it careful thought. I don't give my views lightly, as you well know. Theoretically the experiment was interesting. Fine. The physiologists will be delighted. Moscow will go mad . . . But what is its practical value? What is this creature?' Preobrazhensky pointed toward the consulting room where Sharikov was asleep.

'An unmitigated scoundrel.'

'But what was Klim ... Klim,' cried the professor. 'What was Klim Chugunkin?' (Bormenthal opened his mouth.) 'I'll tell you: two convictions, an alcoholic, "take away all property and divide it up", my beaver hat and twenty roubles gone'— (At this point Philip Philipovich also remembered his presentation walking-stick and turned purple.)—'the swine! ... I'll get that stick back somehow ... In short the pituitary is a magic box which determines the individual human image. Yes, individual ... "... from Granada to Seville ..." ' shouted Philip Philipovich, his eyes rolling furiously, 'but not the universal human image. It's the brain itself in miniature. And it's of no use to me at all—to hell with it. I was concerned about something quite different, about eugenics, about the improvement of the human race. And now I've ended up by specializing in rejuvenation. You don't think I do these rejuvenation operations because of the money, do you? I am a scientist.'

'And a great scientist!' said Bormenthal, gulping down his brandy. His eyes grew bloodshot.

'I wanted to do a little experiment as a follow-up to my success two years ago in extracting sex hormone from the pituitary. Instead of that what has happened? My God! What use were those hormones in the pituitary ... Doctor, I am faced by despair. I confess I am utterly perplexed.'

Suddenly Bormenthal rolled up his sleeves and said, squinting at the tip of his nose:

'Right then, professor, if you don't want to, I will take the risk of dosing him with arsenic myself. I don't care if my father was a plain-clothes policeman under the old regime. When all's said and done this creature is yours—your own experimental creation.'

Philip Philipovich, limp and exhausted, collapsed into his chair and said:

'No, my dear boy, I won't let you do it. I'm sixty, old enough to give you advice. Never do anything criminal, no matter for what reason. Keep your hands clean all your life.'

'But just think, Philip Philipovich, what he may turn into if that character Shvonder keeps on at him! I'm only just beginning to realize what Sharikov may become, by God!'

'Aha, so you realize now, do you? Well *I* realized it ten days after the operation. My only comfort is that Shvonder is the biggest fool of all. He doesn't realize that Sharikov is much more of a threat to him than he is to me. At the moment he's doing all he can to turn Sharikov against me, not realizing that if someone in their turn sets Sharikov against Shvonder himself, there'll soon be nothing left of Shvonder but the bones and the beak.'

'You're right. Just think of the way he goes for cats. He's a man with the heart of a dog.'

'Oh, no, no,' drawled Philip Philipovich in reply. 'You're making a big mistake, doctor. For heaven's sake don't insult the dog. His reaction to cats is purely temporary ... It's a question of discipline, which could be dealt with in two or three weeks, I assure you. Another month or so and he'll stop chasing them.'

'But why hasn't he stopped by now?'

'Elementary, Ivan Arnoldovich ... think what you're saying. After all, the pituitary is not suspended in a vacuum. It is, after all, grafted on to a canine brain, you must allow time for it to take root. Sharikov now only shows traces of canine behaviour and you must remember this—chasing after cats is the *least* objectionable thing he does! The whole horror of the situation is that he now has a *human* heart, not a dog's heart. And about the rottenest heart in all creation!'

Bormenthal, wrought to a state of extreme anxiety, clenched his powerful sinewy hands, shrugged and said firmly:

'Very well, I shall kill him!'

'I forbid it!' answered Philip Philipovich categorically.

'But . . .'

Philip Philipovich was suddenly on the alert. He raised his finger.

'Wait . . . I heard footsteps.'

Both listened intently, but there was silence in the corridor.

'I thought . . .' said Philip Philipovich and began speaking German, several times using the Russian word 'crime'.

'Just a minute,' Bormenthal suddenly warned him and strode over to the door.

Footsteps could be clearly heard approaching the study, and there was a mumble of voices. Bormenthal flung open the door and started back in amazement. Appalled, Philip Philipovich froze in his armchair. In the bright rectangle of the doorway stood Darya Petrovna in nothing but her nightdress, her face hot and furious. Both doctor and professor were dazzled by the amplitude of her powerful body, which their shock caused them to see as naked. Darya Petrovna was dragging something along in her enormous hands and as that 'something' came to a halt it slid down and sat on its bottom. Its short legs, covered in black down, folded up on the parquet floor. The 'something', of course, was Sharikov, confused, still slightly drunk, dishevelled and wearing only a shirt.

Darya Petrovna, naked and magnificent, shook Sharikov like a sack of potatoes and said:

'Just look at our precious lodger Telegraph Telegraphovich. I've been married, but Zina's an innocent girl. It was a good thing I woke up.'

Having said her piece, Darya Petrovna was overcome by shame, gave a scream, covered her bosom with her arms and vanished.

'Darya Petrovna, please forgive us,' the red-faced Philip Philipovich shouted after her as soon as he had regained his senses.

Bormenthal rolled up his shirtsleeves higher still and bore down on Sharikov. Philip Philipovich caught the look in his eye and said in horror: 'Doctor! I forbid you . . .'

With his right hand Bormenthal picked up Sharikov by the scruff of his neck and shook him so violently that the material of his shirt tore.

Philip Philipovich threw himself between them and began to drag the puny Sharikov free from Bormenthal's powerful surgeon's hands.

'You haven't any right to beat me,' said Sharikov in a stifled moan, rapidly sobering as he slumped to the ground.

'Doctor!' shrieked Philip Philipovich.

Bormenthal pulled himself together slightly and let Sharikov go. He at once began to whimper.

'Right,' hissed Bormenthal, 'just wait till tomorrow. I'll fix a little demonstration for him when he sobers up.' With this he grabbed Sharikov under the armpit and dragged him to his bed in the waiting room. Sharikov tried to kick, but his legs refused to obey him.

Philip Philipovich spread his legs wide, sending the skirts of his robe flapping, raised his arms and his eyes towards the lamp in the corridor ceiling and sighed.

Eight

The 'little demonstration' which Bormenthal had promised to lay on for Sharikov did not, however, take place the following morning, because Poligraph Poligraphovich had disappeared from the house. Bormenthal gave way to despair, cursing himself for a fool for not having hidden the key of the front door. Shouting that this was unforgivable, he ended by wishing Sharikov would fall under a bus. Philip Philipovich, who was sitting in his study running his fingers through his hair, said:

'I can just imagine what he must be up to on the street . . . I can just imagine . . . "from Granada to Seville . . ." My God.'

'He may be with the house committee,' said Bormenthal furiously, and dashed off.

At the house committee he swore at the chairman, Shvonder, so violently that Shvonder sat down and wrote a complaint to the local People's Court, shouting as he did so that he wasn't Sharikov's bodyguard. Poligraph Poligraphovich was not very popular at the house committee either, as only yesterday he had taken seven roubles from the funds, with the excuse that he was going to buy textbooks at the cooperative store.

For a reward of three roubles Fyodor searched the whole house from top to bottom. Nowhere was there a trace to be found of Sharikov.

Only one thing was clear—that Poligraph had left at dawn wearing cap, scarf and overcoat, taking with him a bottle of rowanberry brandy from the sideboard, Doctor Bormenthal's gloves, and all his own documents. Darya Petrovna and Zina openly expressed their delight and hoped that Sharikov would never come back again. Sharikov had borrowed fifty roubles from Darya Petrovna only the day before.

'Serve you right!' roared Philip Philipovich, shaking his fists. The telephone rang all that day and all the next day. The doctors saw an unusual number of patients and by the third day the two men were faced with the question of what to tell the police, who would have to start looking for Sharikov in the Moscow underworld.

Hardly had the word 'police' been mentioned than the reverent hush of Obukhov Street was broken by the roar of a lorry and all the windows in the house shook. Then with a confident ring at the bell Poligraph Poligraphovich appeared and entered with an air of unusual dignity. In absolute silence he took off his cap and hung his coat on the hook. He looked completely different. He had on a second-hand leather tunic, worn leather breeches and long English riding-boots laced up to the knee. An incredible odour of cat immediately permeated the whole hall. As though at an unspoken word of command Preobrazhensky and Bormenthal simultaneously crossed their arms, leaned against the doorpost and waited for Poligraph Poligraphovich to make his first remark. He smoothed down his rough hair and cleared his throat, obviously wanting to hide his embarrassment by a nonchalant air.

At last he spoke. 'I've taken a job, Philip Philipovich.'

Both doctors uttered a vague dry noise in the throat and stirred slightly. Preobrazhensky was the first to collect his wits. Stretching out his hand he said: 'Papers.'

The typewritten sheet read: 'It is hereby certified that the bearer, comrade Poligraph Poligraphovich Sharikov, is appointed in charge of the sub-department of the Moscow Cleansing Department responsible for eliminating vagrant quadrupeds (cats, etc.)'

'I see,' said Philip Philipovich gravely. 'Who fixed this for you? No, don't tell me—I can guess.'

'Yes, well, it was Shvonder.'

'Forgive my asking, but why are you giving off such a revolting smell?'

Sharikov anxiously sniffed at his tunic.

'Well, it may smell a bit—that's because of my job. I spent all yesterday strangling cats . . .'

Philip Philipovich shuddered and looked at Bormenthal, whose eyes reminded him of two black gun barrels aimed straight at Sharikov. Without the slightest warning he stepped up to Sharikov and took him in a light, practised grip around the throat.

'Help!' squeaked Sharikov, turning pale.

'Doctor!'

'Don't worry, Philip Philipovich, I shan't do anything violent,' answered Bormenthal in an iron voice and roared: 'Zina and Darya Petrovna!'

The two women appeared in the lobby.

'Now,' said Bormenthal, giving Sharikov's throat a very slight push toward the fur-coat hanging up on a nearby hook, 'repeat after me: "I apologize . . ." ' 'All right, I'll repeat it . . .' replied the defeated Sharikov in a husky voice.

Suddenly he took a deep breath, twisted, and tried to shout 'help', but no sound came out and his head was pushed right into the fur-coat.

'Doctor, please . . .'

Sharikov nodded as a sign that he submitted and would repeat what he had to do.

'... I apologize, dear Darya Petrovna and Zinaida? ...'

'Prokofievna,' whispered Zina nervously.

'Ow ... Prokofievna ... that I allowed myself ...'

'... to behave so disgustingly the other night in a state of intoxication.'

'Intoxication ...'

'I shall never do it again ...'

'Do it again ...'

'Let him go, Ivan Arnoldovich,' begged both women at once. 'You're throttling him.'

Bormenthal released Sharikov and said:

'Is that lorry waiting for you?'

'It just brought me here,' replied Poligraph submissively.

'Zina, tell the driver he can go. Now tell me—have you come back to Philip Philipovich's flat to stay?'

'Where else can I go?' asked Sharikov timidly, his eyes flickering around the room.

'Very well. You will be as good as gold and as quiet as a mouse. Otherwise you will have to reckon with me each time you misbehave. Understand?'

'I understand,' replied Sharikov.

Throughout Bormenthal's attack on Sharikov Philip Philipovich had kept silent. He had leaned against the doorpost with a miserable look, chewed his nails and stared at the floor. Then he suddenly looked up at Sharikov and asked in a toneless, husky voice:

'What do you do with them ... the dead cats, I mean?'

'They go to a laboratory,' replied Sharikov, 'where they make them into protein for the workers.'

After this silence fell on the flat and lasted for two days.

Poligraph Poligraphovich went to work in the morning by truck, returned in the evening and dined quietly with Philip Philipovich and Bormenthal.

Although Bormenthal and Sharikov slept in the same room—the waiting room—they did not talk to each other, which Bormenthal soon found boring.

Two days later, however, there appeared a thin girl wearing eye shadow and pale fawn stockings, very embarrassed by the magnificence of the flat. In her shabby little coat she trotted in behind Sharikov and met the professor in the hall.

Dumbfounded, the professor frowned and asked:

'Who is this?'

'Me and her's getting married. She's our typist. She's coming to live with me. Bormenthal will have to move out of the waiting room. He's got his own flat,' said Sharikov in a sullen and very off-hand voice.

Philip Philipovich blinked, reflected for a moment as he watched the girl turn crimson, then invited her with great courtesy to step into his study for a moment.

'And I'm going with her,' put in Sharikov quickly and suspiciously.

At that moment Bormenthal materialized from the floor.

'I'm sorry,' he said, 'the professor wants to talk to the lady and you and I are going to stay here.'

'I won't,' retorted Sharikov angrily, trying to follow Philip Philipovich and the girl. Her face burned with shame.

'No, I'm sorry,' Bormenthal took Sharikov by the wrist and led him into the consulting room.

For about five minutes nothing was heard from the study, then suddenly came the sound of the girl's muffled sobbing.

Philip Philipovich stood beside his desk as the girl wept into a dirty little lace handkerchief.

'He told me he'd been wounded in the war,' sobbed the girl.

'He's lying,' replied Philip Philipovich inexorably. He shook his head and went on. 'I'm genuinely sorry for you, but you can't just go off and live with the first person you happen to meet at work . . . my dear child, it's scandalous. Here . . .' He opened a desk drawer and took out three ten-rouble notes.

'I'd kill myself,' wept the girl. 'Nothing but salt beef every day in the canteen . . . and he threatened me . . . then he said he'd been a Red Army officer and he'd take me to live in a posh flat . . . kept making passes at me . . . says he's kind-hearted really, he only hates cats . . . He took my ring as a memento . . .'

'Well, well . . . so he's kind-hearted . . . ". . . from Granada to Seville . . ." ' muttered Philip Philipovich. 'You'll get over it, my dear. You're still young.'

'Did you really find him in a doorway?'

'Look, I'm offering to lend you this money—take it,' grunted Philip Philipovich.

The door was then solemnly thrown open and at Philip Philipovich's request Bormenthal led in Sharikov, who glanced shiftily around. The hair on his head stood up like a scrubbing-brush.

'You beast,' said the girl, her eyes flashing, her mascara running past her streakily powdered nose.

'Where did you get that scar on your forehead? Try and explain to the lady,' said Philip Philipovich softly.

Sharikov staked his all on one preposterous card:

'I was wounded at the front fighting against Kolchak,' he barked.

The girl stood up and went out, weeping noisily.

'Stop crying!' Philip Philipovich shouted after her. 'Just a minute—the ring, please,' he said, turning to Sharikov, who obediently removed a large emerald ring from his finger.

'I'll get you,' he suddenly said with malice. 'You'll remember me. Tomorrow I'll make sure they cut your salary.'

'Don't be afraid of him,' Bormenthal shouted after the girl. 'I won't let him do you any harm.' He turned round and gave Sharikov such a look that he stumbled backwards and hit his head on the glass cabinet.

'What's her surname?' asked Bormenthal. 'Her surname!' he roared, suddenly terrible.

'Basnetsova,' replied Sharikov, looking round for a way of escape.

'Every day,' said Bormenthal, grasping the lapels of Sharikov's tunic, 'I shall personally make enquiries at the City Cleansing Department to make sure that you haven't been interfering with citizeness Basnetsova's salary. And if I find out that you have ... then I will shoot you down with my own hands. Take care, Sharikov—I mean what I say.'

Transfixed, Sharikov stared at Bormenthal's nose.

'You're not the only one with a revolver ...' muttered Poligraph quietly.

Suddenly he dodged and spurted for the door.

'Take care!' Bormenthal's shout pursued him as he fled.

That night and the following morning were as tense as the atmosphere before a thunderstorm. Nobody spoke. The next day Poligraph Poligraphovich went gloomily off to work by lorry, after waking up with an uneasy presentiment, while Professor Preobrazhensky saw a former patient, a tall, strapping man in uniform, at a quite abnormal hour. The man insisted on a consultation and was admitted. As he walked into the study he politely clicked his heels to the professor.

'Have your pains come back?' asked Philip Philipovich pursing his lips. 'Please sit down.'

'Thank you. No, professor,' replied his visitor, putting down his cap on the edge of the desk. 'I'm very grateful to you ... No ... I've come, hm, on another matter, Philip Philipovich ... in view of the great respect I feel ... I've come to ... er, warn you. It's obviously nonsense, of course. He's simply a scoundrel.' The patient searched in his briefcase and took out a piece of paper. 'It's a good thing I was told about this right away ...'

Philip Philipovich slipped a pince-nez over his spectacles and began to read. For a long time he mumbled half-aloud, his expression changing every moment. '... also threatening to murder the chairman of the house committee, comrade Shvonder, which shows that he must be keeping a firearm. And he makes counter-revolutionary speeches. and even ordered his domestic worker, Zinaida Prokofievna Bunina, to burn Engels in the stove. He is an obvious Menshevik and so is his assistant Ivan Arnoldovich Bormenthal who is living secretly in his flat without being registered.

Signed: *P. P. Sharikov*
        Sub-Dept. Controller
        City Cleansing Dept.
Countersigned: *Shvonder*
        Chairman, House Committee.
        Pestrukhin
        Secretary, House Committee.

'May I keep this?' asked Philip Philipovich, his face blotchy.

'Or perhaps you need it so that legal proceedings can be made?'

'Really, professor.' The patient was most offended and blew out his nostrils. 'You seem to regard us with contempt. I ...' And he began to puff himself up like a turkeycock.

'Please forgive me, my dear fellow!' mumbled Philip Philipovich. 'I really didn't mean to offend you. Please don't be angry. You can't believe what this creature has done to my nerves . . .'

'So I can imagine,' said the patient, quite mollified. 'But what a swine! I'd be curious to have a look at him. Moscow is full of stories about you . . .'

Philip Philipovich could only gesture in despair. It was then that the patient noticed how hunched the professor was looking and that he seemed to have recently grown much greyer.

Nine

The crime ripened, then fell like a stone, as usually happens. With an uncomfortable feeling round his heart Poligraph Poligraphovich returned that evening by lorry. Philip Philipovich's voice invited him into the consulting room. Surprised, Sharikov entered and looked first, vaguely frightened, at Bormenthal's steely face, then at Philip Philipovich. A cloud of smoke surrounded the doctor's head and his left hand, trembling very slightly, held a cigarette and rested on the shiny handle of the obstetrical chair.

With ominous calm Philip Philipovich said:

'Go and collect your things at once—trousers, coat, everything you need—then get out of this flat!'

'What is all this?' Sharikov was genuinely astonished.

'Get out of this flat—and today,' repeated Philip Philipovich, frowning down at his fingernails.

An evil spirit was at work inside Poligraph Poligraphovich. It was obvious that his end was in sight and his time nearly up, but he hurled himself towards the inevitable and barked in an angry staccato:

'Like hell I will! You got to give me my rights. I've a right to thirty-seven square feet and I'm staying right here.'

'Get out of this flat,' whispered Philip Philipovich in a strangled voice.

It was Sharikov himself who invited his own death. He raised his left hand, which stank most horribly of cats, and cocked a snook at Philip Philipovich. Then with his right hand he drew a revolver on Bormenthal. Bormenthal's cigarette fell like a shooting star. A few seconds later Philip Philipovich was hopping about on broken glass and running from the cabinet to the couch. On it, spreadeagled and croaking, lay a sub-department controller of the City Cleansing Department; Bormenthal the surgeon was sitting astride his chest and suffocating him with a small white pad.

After some minutes Bormenthal, with a most unfamiliar look, walked out on to the landing and stuck a notice beside the doorbell:

The Professor regrets that owing to indisposition he will be unable to hold consulting hours today. Please do not disturb the Professor by ringing the bell.

With a gleaming penknife he then cut the bell-cable, inspected his scratched and bleeding face in the mirror and his lacerated, slightly trembling hands. Then he went into the kitchen and said to the anxious Zina and Darya Petrovna:

'The professor says you mustn't leave the flat on any account.'

'No, we won't,' they replied timidly.

'Now I must lock the back door and keep the key,' said Bormenthal, sidling round the room and covering his face with his hand. 'It's only temporary, not because we don't trust you. But if anybody came you might not be able to keep them out and we mustn't be disturbed. We're busy.'

'All right,' replied the two women, turning pale. Bormenthal locked the back door, locked the front door, locked the door from the corridor into the hall and his footsteps faded away into the consulting room.

Silence filled the flat, flooding into every corner. Twilight crept in, dank and sinister and gloomy. Afterwards the neighbours across the courtyard said that every light burned that evening in the windows of Preobrazhensky's consulting room and that they even saw the professor's white skullcap ... It is hard to be sure. When it was all over Zina did say, though, that when Bormenthal and the professor emerged from the consulting room, there, by the study fireplace, Ivan Arnoldovich had frightened her to death. It seems he was squatting down in front of the fire and burning one of the blue-bound notebooks which contained the medical notes on the professor's patients. The doctor's face, apparently, was quite green and completely—yes, completely—scratched to pieces. And that evening Philip Philipovich had been most peculiar. And then there was another thing—but maybe that innocent girl from the flat in Prechistenka Street was talking rubbish ...

One thing, though, was certain: there was silence in the flat that evening—total, frightening silence.

Epilogue

One night, exactly ten days to the day after the struggle in Professor Preobrazhensky's consulting room in his flat on Obukhov Street, there was a sharp ring of the doorbell.

'Criminal police. Open up, please.'

Footsteps approached, people knocked and entered until a considerable crowd filled the brightly lit waiting room with its newly glazed cabinet. There were two in police uniform, one in a black overcoat and carrying a briefcase; there was chairman Shvonder, pale and gloating, and the youth who had turned out to be a woman; there was Fyodor the porter, Zina, Darya Petrovna and Bormenthal, half dressed and embarrassed as he tried to cover up his tieless neck.

The door from the study opened to admit Philip Philipovich. He appeared in his familiar blue dressing gown and everybody could tell at once that over the past week Philip Philipovich had begun to look very much better. The old Philip Philipovich, masterful, energetic and dignified, now faced his nocturnal visitors and apologized for appearing in his dressing gown.

'It doesn't matter, professor,' said the man in civilian clothes, in great embarrassment. He faltered and then said: 'I'm sorry to say we have a warrant to search your flat and'— the men stared uneasily at Philip Philipovich's moustaches and ended: 'to arrest you, depending on the results of our search.'

Philip Philipovich frowned and asked:

'What, may I ask, is the charge, and who is being charged?'

The man scratched his cheek and began reading from a piece of paper from his briefcase.

'Preobrazhensky, Bormenthal, Zinaida Bunina and Darya Ivanova are charged with the murder of Poligraph Poligraphovich Sharikov, sub-department controller, City of Moscow Cleansing Department.'

The end of his speech was drowned by Zina's sobs. There was general movement.

'I don't understand,' replied Philip Philipovich with a regal shrug. 'Who is this Sharikov? Oh, of course, you mean my dog . . . the one I operated on?'

'I'm sorry, professor, not a dog. This happened when he was a man. That's the trouble.'

'Because he talked?' asked Philip Philipovich. 'That doesn't mean he was a man. Anyhow, it's irrelevant. Sharik is alive at this moment and no one has killed him.'

'Really, professor?' said the man in black, deeply astonished, and raised his eyebrows. 'In that case you must produce him. It's ten days now since he disappeared and the evidence, if you'll forgive my saying so, is most disquieting.'

'Doctor Bormenthal, will you please produce Sharik for the detective,' ordered Philip Philipovich, pocketing the charge-sheet. Bormenthal went out, smiling enigmatically.

As he returned he gave a whistle and from the door into the study appeared a dog of the most extraordinary appearance. In patches he was bald, while in other patches his coat had grown. He entered like a trained circus dog walking on his hind legs, then dropped on to all fours and looked round. The waiting room froze into a sepulchral silence as tangible as jelly. The nightmarish-looking dog with the crimson scar on the forehead stood up again on his hind legs, grinned and sat down in an armchair.

The second policeman suddenly crossed himself with a sweeping gesture and in stepping back knocked Zina's legs from under her.

The man in black, his mouth still wide open, said:

'What's been going on? . . . He worked in the City Cleansing Department . . .'

'I didn't send him there,' answered Philip Philipovich. 'He was recommended for the job by Mr Shvonder, if I'm not mistaken.'

'I don't get it,' said the man in black, obviously confused, and turned to the first policeman. 'Is that him?'

'Yes,' whispered the policeman, 'it's him all right.'

'That's him,' came Fyodor's voice, 'except the little devil's got a bit fatter.'

'But he talked . . .' the man in black giggled nervously.

'And he still talks, though less and less, so if you want to hear him talk now's the time, before he stops altogether.'

'But why?' asked the man in black quietly.

Philip Philipovich shrugged his shoulders.

'Science has not yet found the means of turning animals into people. I tried, but unsuccessfully, as you can see. He talked and then he began to revert back to his primitive state. Atavism.'

'Don't swear at me,' the dog suddenly barked from his chair and stood up.

The man in black turned instantly pale, dropped his briefcase and began to fall sideways. A policeman caught him on one side and Fyodor supported him from behind. There was a sudden turmoil, clearly pierced by three sentences:

Philip Philipovich: 'Give him valerian. He's fainted.'

Doctor Bormenthal: 'I shall personally throw Shvonder downstairs if he ever appears in Professor Preobrazhensky's flat again.'

And Shvonder said: 'Please enter that remark in the report.'

The grey accordion-shaped radiators hissed gently. The blinds shut out the thick Prechistenka Street night sky with its lone star. The great, the powerful benefactor of dogs sat in his chair while Sharik lay stretched out on the carpet beside the leather couch. In the mornings the March fog made the dog's head ache, especially around the circular scar on his skull, but by evening the warmth banished the pain. Now it was easing all the time and warm, comfortable thoughts flowed through the dog's mind.

I've been very, very lucky, he thought sleepily. Incredibly lucky. I'm really settled in this flat. Though I'm not so sure now about my pedigree. Not a drop of labrador blood. She was just a tart, my old grandmother, God rest her soul. Certainly they cut my head around a bit, but who cares. None of my business, really.

From the distance came a tinkle of glass. Bormenthal was tidying the shelves of the cabinet in the consulting room.

The grey-haired magician sat and hummed: ' ". . . to the banks of the sacred Nile . . ." '

That evening the dog saw terrible things. He saw the great man plunge his slippery, rubber-gloved hands into a jar to fish out a brain; then relentlessly, persistently the great man pursued his search. Slicing, examining, he frowned and sang:

' "To the banks of the sacred Nile . . ." '